THE 3RD OPTION

PRAISE FOR THE SECOND EDITION OF
THE 3RD OPTION

"This is one of the most enjoyable works of fiction I've ever read.

"I won't spoil the plot, but it involves an emerging technology that has the potential to effectively SOLVE one of the most divisive political issues of our time. It's a relatively unknown technology with ramifications for the entire political status quo, and this book is a wonderfully entertaining awareness-raising vehicle.

"Kudos, Ben! Thanks for helping nudge this important issue onto the center stage, and for crafting such an engaging story around it."

—Matt Deaton, PhD, adjunct philosophy professor at The University of Texas at Tyler, and author of *Abortion Ethics in a Nutshell: A Pro-Both Tour of the Moral Arguments*

"Every so often a work of fiction speaks uniquely to the heart of a divisive societal issue. Such is the case with *The 3rd Option*, authored by Ben A. Sharpton. This fast-moving novel offers a surprising paradigm shift from the usual 'pro-life, pro-choice' dichotomy within a storyline of an underlying violence, greed, and deceit.

"This is an excellent read offering valuable and relevant insight."

—Dr. Bob Ayres, Anglican priest, consultant, and author of *DEAFCHURCH 21: Vision for a New Generation*

"This is the kind of rare thriller that I love—one that grabs you on page one and won't let you go until the satisfying conclusion. *The 3rd Option* is smart and fresh, combining timely issues with thoughtful insights, relatable characters, and shocking twists. It makes you think while it makes your heart race."

—Peter Wallace, author of *A Generous Beckoning* and host emeritus of Day1

PRAISE FOR THE FIRST EDITION OF
THE 3ᴿᴰ OPTION

First place in the action category of the Readers' Favorite contest

Winner of the Reader Views Literary Award for the southeast region

Honorable mention in the action and adventure category
of the ForeWord Book of the Year contest

Winner of the urban/edgy category in the Chanticleer
Reviews Paranormal Book contest

Finalist in the suspense/thriller and second novel categories
for the Next Generation Indie Book Awards

Finalist in the suspense category of the Indie Excellence Award

THE 3RD OPTION

OPTION

BEN A. SHARPTON

BELLE ISLE BOOKS
www.belleislebooks.com

ISBN: 978-1-958754-95-5

Library of Congress Control Number: 2023917633

Printed in the United States

Published by:

BELLE ISLE BOOKS
www.belleislebooks.com

In memory of Mom, who loved every child she ever met, and in gratitude to my wife and family for making time for me to put my thoughts on paper.

In hopes that we can all learn to negotiate and compromise once again and find new options to resolve our issues and conflicts.

ONE

It was just a job interview, nothing more.

Still, anticipation tickled the back of Allan Chappel's neck as he headed up the walk toward the offices of Inc.Ubator, the medical think tank his old grad school friend Dan Carlisle had recently opened. Good fortune was coming his way after a long period of absence.

This job had to be better than the one he held now, writing press releases, PR material, and employee meeting scripts for a regional building supply retailer. Dan had shared just a bit of the exciting technology his team was exploring, but it was enough to get Allan pumped. Life-saving medical supplies, technologies, and cutting-edge procedures trumped wallboard, wood putty, and water faucets any day.

Dan had said this job would give him a chance to change the world, a dream Allan had back when they were in school at Emory: Allan in seminary and Dan in med school. But things had changed, people had died, and Allan had traded his clerical collar for a corporate cubicle. He'd turned his back on a life of purpose for one of simple subsistence.

He straightened his tie over his tight shirt collar. No, this was more than a job interview. It opened a doorway to meaning in his life. For the first time in a long, long time, Allan was excited about the future. It was faint, almost unreal, but he felt he could reach out and touch it.

On the other side of the parking lot, two men were in the middle of a furious argument, apparently about a bumper sticker on one of the men's cars. The two were face-to-face, and the hot afternoon sun threatened to raise their argument to near-nuclear levels. Allan stayed on his side of the lot, lest they draw him into their escalating fight. As he watched the argument get more heated, Allan felt as if the entire world was heading over a cliff, lemming-like.

Allan turned away from the chaos in the parking lot and toward the hope represented by the organization in the office complex before him. Halfway up the walk, Allan stumbled on a raised chunk of sidewalk. He knelt down and examined his scuffed shoe, cursing his clumsiness. Moistening his fingertips with his tongue, he tried to rub away the scratches on the toe of his Rockfords.

Leaping up the front steps, he reached for the handle on the massive door. As he began to pull the door open, his march into the future was interrupted by a rumble that came from deep beneath his feet. He paused, his hand feeling the vibration from the door as his eyes were accosted with a bright flash of light. The building that had been his beacon to a brighter tomorrow exploded, and Allan's thoughts faded to nothingness.

"You are the luckiest son of a bitch I've seen in a long time." A big man with a chasm between his front teeth stood beside Allan's bed when he awoke.

"Huh?" Allan fought his way out of a thick fog of medication and confusion to focus on the lanky man beside his bed.

"You know, you should be dead, for all intents and purposes," the man said. He wore a brown plaid sports jacket and an ugly tie that he must have selected in the dark of night because the two came nowhere close to matching.

Allan's thoughts became clearer now, and with that came a good dose of cynicism. "Being dead wasn't my intent or purpose," he said. He groaned and shifted his weight on the emergency room bed. He felt sore, aching in places he had never ached before. A flimsy curtain separated his bed from others nearby. He could hear voices coming from outside his sterile environment.

"What's your name, son?" Mr. Ugly Tie said.

"Allan Chappel."

"Mr. Chappel, I'm Inspector Johnson."

Allan started to nod, but a brace that had been clamped around his neck by some unknown paramedic a few hours earlier prevented much movement. "Uh-huh," Allan mumbled.

"So, Mr. Chappel. What brought you to that family planning clinic this afternoon?"

"I don't know what you're talking about."

"The family planning clinic on Northside Drive. That's where the paramedics found you."

"Mr. Johnson, you're, uh, mistaken," Allan said, his voice thick and low. "That office wasn't a clinic. It was a medical think tank."

Inspector Johnson frowned, bringing his bushy eyebrows together like twin caterpillars. "According to the licensing department, it's a family planning clinic. Who told you it was a—what did you call it? A medical think tank?"

Allan groaned. As the medication wore off, his head hurt more, and the inspector's inane questions weren't helping a bit. "Dr. Dan Carlisle, CEO of Inc.Ubator," Allan said.

"Carlisle?"

"Yeah, Carlisle. Son of Congressman James Carlisle. Dan invited me to interview for a PR job there."

Johnson scribbled in his notepad. "What did Dr. Carlisle say they did at this facility?"

"We hadn't gotten into it very much. They were developing new, progressive ideas for the medical industry," Allan said. "He claimed to have experts around the country working with him. I met with Dan and some of his staff this morning. They wanted me to talk with one of their consultants, a psychiatrist named Chamberlain, over on Peachtree. I filled out some surveys and inventories and stuff, and then I went back to their offices." He felt as if he were coming out of a dream—a very bad dream. The questions and thinking worked together to wake him up. His mind became clearer. His headache pounded harder.

"How well did you know this Carlisle fella?" the inspector asked.

"Not very well, at least not recently," Allan said. "We knew each other in grad school. He was in med school. I was in seminary."

"Why would a preacher apply for a job at an abortion clinic?" Johnson's slow drawl dragged the sentence out much longer than necessary. His insistent reference to the office as a clinic annoyed Allan. It was obvious the inspector had made up his mind, and he wouldn't consider anything else.

Allan shook his head. "No. I dropped out of seminary." He added, slowly drawing out each word, one after the other: "It ... was ... not ... a ... clinic."

Johnson stared into Allan's eyes. "Ever hear of Eric Rudolph, activist back in the nineties? Bombed an abortion clinic right here in Atlanta. How about that guy who burned down the clinic in Knoxville last New Year's Eve? Are you sure you've got nothing you wanna tell me, Mr. Chappel?"

Allan knew what the inspector was insinuating, and he didn't like it. "Hell no, I don't have anything I wanna tell you," he mimicked. "I knew Dan Carlisle a long time ago. He asked me to interview for a job. I went to see the consultant as part of the interview process. When I came back, the place exploded, and I woke up here with you asking questions."

Allan felt jittery, like he'd downed too many espressos too fast, which only made the inspector's slow speech patterns even more annoying. He began to remember details as adrenaline pumped into his brain. He recalled snippets of scenes that had taken place after the explosion. People were screaming. The stench of smoke filled his lungs. Some kids tried to grab pieces of the building as souvenirs while police officers worked to keep the gathering crowd back. A broad-shouldered bald man, his chin covered by a jet-black goatee beneath a flat nose that looked to have been bent by considerable force, seemed to stare at him as someone might stare at a classmate years after graduation. Allan tried to shake off the haze in his mind as he realized the gravity of the situation. Things were bad and quickly sliding toward worse.

Johnson cocked his head and stared at Allan, like a dog trying to discern an unusual sound. He handed a business card to Allan. "Now listen, Mr. Chappel. If you think of anything, anything at all that might help us in this case, you give me a call, ya hear?"

"Yeah."

"I'm sure the doctor will be here in a few moments," he said as he drew the curtain aside and slipped out.

Allan lay back and took a deep breath, trying to shake the mixture of fog and tension, but his thoughts were interrupted by the vibrations of his cell phone, which still lay nestled in his pocket.

U R in danger. Get away. As always, Aunt Julia's text message was short and to the point—urgency punctuated by brevity.

Allan had learned long ago to trust her messages as if they came from God, Himself. Sitting up in bed, he tugged the brace from around his neck, clambered out of bed, and slipped to the curtain entrance. At the registration window, a soccer mom, her ponytail dangling through the back of an Atlanta Braves baseball cap, was arguing about how long she had been in the waiting room with her child. Allan took advantage of the distraction and strolled almost nonchalantly toward the emergency room exit.

Northside Hospital was a conglomeration of structures that seemed to have grown, cancer-like, over the years, as new medical needs for new patients were discovered. The growth continued even now, resulting in temporary fencing, roadblocks, and detour signs throughout the complex. Allan hurried through the construction junk and medical office parks toward the retail area of the city. He tried his best to look like a normal thirty-something adult strolling down the street.

He passed shops and parking garages. Two blocks away from the hospital, he tried to jog, not sure what he was running from but sensing Aunt Julia was right. The pain of his bruised muscles forced him to slow back to a walk. His heart pounding in his ears, he turned at the next street and stumbled through a crowd of people coming out of a bar. He crossed the street and continued his pilgrimage through a little park nestled between two buildings. His breath came hard, and he cursed himself for not spending more time at the gym.

With each step, a dart of pain stabbed his skull, but he continued to walk away from the hospital, the strange police inspector, and the dangers they represented.

Leaning into the wind, he was aware of cars racing by on the street bordering the walk. Their owners were going home, rushing to get out of traffic, away from the office, and back to nice houses filled with loving families, warm food, and a pet or two. He envied them.

Daylight was waning, and with it, what little warmth the fall air still held. The coming darkness made him feel even more vulnerable.

He had to get home, where he could relax, regroup, and figure out his next steps. He decided to call Aunt Julia to seek her advice. Pulling his phone from his pocket, he flicked it on.

A powerful force rammed into his side, throwing the phone from his fingers and pushing him into the rough brick masonry of a nearby office building. He bounced, bleeding, from the wall only to be punched in the face by a steel fist. He dropped to his knees onto the wet bricks of a dark alley, knowing this was not the place he wanted to be during an attack. Looking up, he saw that the alley opened onto a street a hundred feet away. His hand brushed against his phone, which had clattered to the ground beside him. He grabbed it and sprinted toward the exit, his body screaming in pain with each step.

His attacker seemed caught off guard by Allan's fast retreat, as if he hadn't expected him to get up so fast. He uttered a low mumble and sprinted after the fleeing man.

Allan burst out of the alley into the dimming light of dusk. He could hear his assailant breathing like a locomotive behind him. He turned left and ran up a little hill as fast as his pained body would allow. The sidewalk was fairly empty, but people in passing vehicles stared. "Help!" he yelled, hoping someone would call the police.

A hand grabbed at his left shoulder, but he jerked to the right and avoided capture. He managed to cross the street, just a couple of steps ahead of the man chasing him. He turned right and found it easier to head downhill. A cool wind blew through his long brown hair.

But the guy behind him was running faster downhill as well.

"Help!" Allan yelled again, but no one came to his rescue.

Just as he was about to turn right and head back across the street, the man caught up to him and threw him like a rag doll into a pile of boxes and trashcans in another alley. This alley was much shorter than the other and opened onto a busy thoroughfare crowded with speeding traffic.

"Allan Chappel?" a thick, raspy voice echoed from somewhere in the dim backstreet. "Are you Allan Chappel?"

"Er, uh, what?" Allan coughed. "You can have my wallet."

The bald guy standing before him snorted. His distorted nose, flat against his face, made the rest of his head seem enormous. Allan stared at his face and realized that this was the big man he had seen outside of the Inc.Ubator office just before it exploded.

"I don't want your wallet," the man's lips said from beneath his black mustache. "You shouldn't have been late for your appointment." His fist drew back, ready to strike again. Allan rolled into a ball, trying desperately to protect himself, aware that there was no way in hell he could.

In an instant Allan knew he'd been targeted. Something about this man, his knowledge of Allan's name, and his intense pursuit chilled Allan to the bone and made him ache even more.

Then the bald man stopped.

For a second, Allan felt relief. But only for a second.

Sensing the coming doom, he struggled as his attacker dragged him upright and toward the street and the rushing traffic at the other end of the alley. The man pulled Allan's body close to his as his mighty arms drew back, preparing to cast the smaller man into the nearby street, like a fisherman might cast a lure into a rushing river. Allan could smell his stale breath. His cheek brushed against the man's beard. His attacker's shirt opened to reveal an intricate tattoo of an eagle, holding arrows in one claw and an olive branch in the other, adorning his left breast. Allan flailed against the bald man, trying to break free from his grasp, trying to find a way to survive and avoid the oncoming tragedy.

In one mighty motion, the bald man burst from the alley, pushing Allan's body before him. "Errrruuhhhhhgg," he shouted as he rushed toward the street.

Allan felt his body leave the pavement and soar backwards through the air. Automobile headlights blinded his eyes. He threw his left arm over his chest, twisting his body around in an attempt to right himself. The squeal of tires screamed in the night as an oncoming driver slammed on brakes to avoid him. The car stopped inches away.

Allan's feet touched the ground long enough to bounce his swirling frame farther into the street. He heard a loud bang and, for a second, thought he had been shot by the bald man, who was now slinking back into the dark alley. When the car before him hurtled forward, he realized it had been rear-ended by the vehicle behind it. He somehow noticed, in his adrenaline-fueled, slow-motion state, that the car was a black BMW. It plowed into his hip, flinging his legs and feet over his head. He rolled onto the hood and glimpsed the shocked face of the lady behind the wheel, holding a cell phone to her ear and watching as his helpless body hurtled toward her. He felt his shoulder crack into the windshield before his body bounced into the air and onto the top of her car.

He slid down the back of the BMW and onto the hood of an SUV, now melded into the BMW's trunk.

"Are you all right?" someone shouted.

"Call the police," someone else yelled.

Allan stumbled back onto the sidewalk, looking for the bald man, trying to avoid him, trying to run away from him.

Pain flashed through his hip every time his left foot hit the ground. He couldn't stop to lick his wounds. He had to get away.

He ran up the street, away from the accident, the traffic, and the bald man with the intricate chest tattoo. At that point he realized he had somehow managed to hang onto his cell phone. The initial loss, when he had dropped it in the alley, must have caused him to hold on to it tightly after he retrieved it. He stuffed it in his pocket, glad to have a lifeline for use later.

But at the moment, he ran. Pain throbbed in his hip and shoulder, tempting him to stop, but he ran. The cold air seared his lungs, but he ran. He couldn't do anything else.

———————————

He stopped.

This part of Atlanta rippled with upscale shopping centers and strip malls, packed with virtually every name-brand retail outlet ever conceived. Brilliant spotlights, streetlights, and car lights were everywhere, making him feel as conspicuous as a black moth on a white curtain. He found a bank and withdrew the daily limit of cash, knowing it might come in handy. The money provided him with a tiny sense of security, allowing him to slow down. He used his phone to request an Uber.

He confirmed he had the right car and hunched low in the back seat as the car took him through the city. Safe and secure, he dialed Aunt Julia's number.

Allan's grandfather had always said Aunt Julia was as crazy as a bat. Truth be told, Allan knew she wasn't. He'd taken enough pastoral counseling courses in seminary to understand that she was not clinically insane. Not quite. But she was different.

She had come of age in the sixties and somehow stayed there, suspended in time. Now in her early seventies, she still wore long, flowing, flower-print sundresses, even in the dead of winter, which never was that dead in Arizona. It was as if the natural spiritual influence that seemed pervasive in hippie communes had somehow blended with the ancient feeling of the surrounding landscape and come to nest and rest with Aunt Julia.

She was also psychic. At least, that was what she had told him since he was a little boy.

When she visited his family in Tampa—they never visited her in Arizona—she would whisper tidbits that always seemed to come true into his ear. "You're going to be very happy with your report card," she had said, and a week later he received straight A grades. "Guard your left eye," she had said two days before he was hit in the helmet by a sidearm pitcher in a Little League baseball game. The coach said that if he hadn't lowered his head, he might have suffered permanent damage to that eye. "Have you picked out your tux, yet?" she had asked a few weeks before his best friend talked him into taking Kathy Barker to the prom.

Crazy as a bat? No. But maybe gifted.

"Allan," she answered. Her voice sounded warm and familiar, and yet older and frail. "I'm so glad you called. Are you all right?"

"Right now I am. I had a couple of very close calls a few hours ago."

"I knew it, Allan. I knew something was very wrong."

"Thank you for the warning."

"You're not free from danger yet," she quickly added. "There are strong forces working against you."

"Okay. I'll be careful. Is there anything I should look out for?"

"You know the images are never that clear. I just know that someone is trying to hurt you. He is tenacious. He will not stop until he succeeds."

Aunt Julia was beginning to get preachy. "I'll be on my guard, Aunt Julia."

"Please do, Allan. You know, you and I have a bond. I've never sensed the spiritual space about anyone as much as I have you."

"I'm grateful for that."

"Stay in touch, my angel."

"You too."

They never talked long. They didn't have to.

TWO

The house seemed darker than usual. It may have been that Allan was comparing it to the brilliantly lit shops and strip malls where he had caught the cab. It may have been the late hour. Or, it may have been the situation that made everything around him seem dark, empty, and bleak.

Allan unlocked the back door, entered the kitchen, and switched on the fluorescent light. Feeling dizzy, he grabbed a chair to steady himself. "What a fuckin' day," he said aloud. Realizing he hadn't eaten since breakfast, he made a beeline to the refrigerator.

The fridge was almost empty, as usual. Last week's Chinese food was about to grow legs and walk away. Two of the three glass shelves held nothing but leftover ketchup spills. The cheese in one of the drawers had more hair than that bald guy's goatee.

Thoughts of the bald guy made him freeze up again. He couldn't relax. He realized it was possible the bald man could have come to his home. After all, he had been targeted. The bald man had used his name in the alley and expected him to be in the Inc.Ubator office when it exploded. He may also have Allan's home address.

Allan didn't own a gun—not even a knife for protection. He looked in the closet for a potential weapon. It was almost as empty as the refrigerator. He took an old mop but paused when he considered swinging it at the threatening bald guy. He ran it through the space between the back door and the doorframe, between the hinges. Leaning back with all of his weight, he snapped the handle off the mop, giving him a staff of sorts that might be used to stab or strike an assailant.

Armed with his makeshift weapon, he crept into the back of the house. In his gut, he knew he wasn't safe.

Seeking security, he decided to call the inspector. He pulled the business card from his pocket and grabbed the kitchen phone. When his fingers hovered over the keys of the cordless phone, he realized they were shaking almost uncontrollably.

"This is Inspector Johnson of the Atlanta police," the thick voice of the inspector announced.

"Inspector Johnson, this is Allan Chappel. I've been attacked by a big, bald man with a black goatee. He followed me from the hospital and tried to kill me." Allan chose not to mention that he left the hospital before seeing a doctor.

"Take it easy, son," Johnson said.

"He knew I was interviewing at the Inc.Ubator office and tried to take me out."

"I'm sorry, did you say he was trying to take you out?"

Allan's cheeks burned. "Look," he said. "This guy is trying to kill me. He was at the Inc.Ubator offices this afternoon."

"Where are you now, boy?"

"I'm at home, but I don't feel very safe here. He may have followed me."

"I'm sure you'll be just fine," Johnson continued. "I'll send a patrol car by your house to pick you up and plan to meet you at the office. Give me about thirty minutes. You may feel better if you stay in a motel tonight. We can talk about that at the police station."

"Thank you, sir."

"The patrol car will be there in a few minutes. You'll be okay."

Allan hung up the phone, feeling better than he'd felt all night. He grabbed a backpack and stuffed some clothes inside. Diving into the bedroom closet, he fished out his fireproof safe. From the bottom of the safe, he grabbed an envelope containing about a thousand dollars in cash—his emergency stash. He threw the envelope into the backpack.

He returned to search the refrigerator. The milk didn't smell too bad, so he poured some in a bowl of Cheerios and shoveled it down with a soup spoon while he collected the rest of his gear.

The events of the day seemed to drift away, almost like a nightmare. He felt himself winding down like a broken clock. The house was silent. But inside, he knew something was terribly wrong. The milk was not right. He felt woozy.

The only noise was the loud crunching sound in his ears that came from each bite of cereal. The sound became louder. There were just a couple of beige Cheerios left floating leisurely in a pool of milk at the bottom of the bowl. They glided together and bumped into each other, and the noise of their collision echoed through the house.

He carried the bowl to the sink. Every step sounded like a slow-motion sledgehammer pounding on metal. He looked up into the dark window above the sink and saw the reflection of the bald man standing behind him. Allan's eyesight grew foggy, and he began to see the man's lips as a large Cheerio. Allan dropped the bowl in the sink and heard it land with a thundering crash.

Turning, he grabbed the broken mop handle and swung it like a baseball bat. His aim was far off, and each swing seemed to take forever. The room tilted, and he struggled to stand upright. The bald man with the crooked nose laughed at him through his Cheerios lips.

Allan pulled the handle in and pointed it at his foe like a sword.

"Ooh. Now I'm scared, little Allan," he taunted. "Did you like your milk and cereal?"

Floating up through his mental haze, the thought that the bald man might have doctored his milk made Allan angry. He jabbed his mop handle toward the man's chest, but the big brute just knocked the makeshift spear away. Allan jabbed again, but he missed his mark when the bald man moved sideways. The man was fast . . . or Allan was incredibly slow.

Allan was dizzy, and his knees felt weak. He drew the mop handle back beside his head and threw it as hard as he could, like a javelin. To his amazement, the bald man caught it in mid-air, broke it over his knee, and tossed it aside.

The bald man came closer and reached for Allan's arm. Allan hit him as hard as he could with his other fist, but the bald man just laughed. His powerful fingers closed around Allan's arm, and Allan threw up milk and cereal all over the eagle tattoo on the man's chest.

Joseph P. Strong was pissed.

He stormed out the entrance to the Augusta Grande Hotel with his faithful head of security and personal bodyguard, Tom Gaines, in tow. The LifeWatch annual celebration dinner had been a bust. Usually, two or three hundred supporters, dressed to the nines in tuxedoes and elaborate gowns, would have been seated at round dining tables filling the ornate banquet room, but tonight, no more than sixty-five were in attendance, and almost fifty people dropped out at the last minute. LifeWatch, the organization he had founded twenty years earlier, would lose a wad of cash on this fundraiser. He knew without checking that the gifts would be abysmal. Many of the donated items for the silent auction wouldn't even receive one bid.

This was bad.

Even though LifeWatch was large for a nonprofit, it was not impervious to financial hardship. The drop in this year's income—from this event, online donations, and special grants—would undoubtedly cripple the organization's operations. They'd have to cut back on their video commercial production, regional rallies, and even funds they used to support like-minded politicians. They might even have to chop heads in their telephone call center. It was going to be ugly.

"You had a masterful performance this evening, sir," Gaines offered.

The tall, trim president of LifeWatch turned to confront his bodyguard. "To a room full of empty chairs," he said, glaring down the shorter employee.

"I understand that we didn't have the kind of crowds we used to have ..."

"We had larger turnouts during the pandemic," Strong countered. "They filled that hall, wearing those hideously stupid masks, but they were there."

"I was just suggesting that your part was excellent, as usual."

"A lot of good that does."

Gaines stood at attention, silently.

"Ever since that ill-timed decision last summer by the Supremes ..."

"Ill-timed?"

"Of course! They could have waited until the mid-terms were over. We always get a huge financial bump during an election year, but they had to move early, and that screwed everything up. Now, our giving will be way below our budget, and our work will suffer." Then the idea just came to him. "We will just have to bring in some big guns to draw more people."

Their intense conversation was interrupted when a woman, dressed in a beautiful, ornate gown that was adorned tastefully with sequins, approached them as her husband talked with the valet. "Excuse me, Dr. Strong? Pardon me ... I just want you to know how very much I—er—we, my husband and I, appreciate what you do."

Dr. Strong smiled and said, "Well, thank you so much." He turned to introduce her to Tom. "This is Tom Gaines, the head of security at LifeWatch."

"I'm so glad to meet you," Tom said, extending his hand. It was a social play, a strategy in which Tom coerced her to say her name, so Joseph would hear it and not be embarrassed by the fact that he had no idea who she was. "And you are?"

She seemed flattered that he asked. "I'm Elizabeth Bridges. My friends call me Beth Ann. That's my husband by the car." She motioned to the valet stand.

Joseph took control of the conversation from here. "Beth Ann, it's so nice to see you tonight."

"We attend this celebration every year," she continued. "I know you've had much larger crowds in previous years, and I hope tonight's attendance won't discourage you."

"Oh, no ma'am. Not at all."

"That's good. It must be comforting to know that our country is changing for the better. Since so much has happened lately, especially here in Georgia, to protect the unborn, it seems like we are finally making real progress. You must be pleased." She stopped talking and stared at the two men as if waiting for an answer.

Strong took a deep breath. "We are proud of what this organization has accomplished. However, we can't rest on our successes. There are other states that don't share our beliefs and values, so it's important for us to keep fighting to share our message with them."

"That may be so, but now that the problem has been resolved in Georgia, my husband and I have started looking at some of the other evil practices around us. We're particularly concerned about the books our children are checking out in our local public library. They are truly despicable. Does LifeWatch have any programs to help keep those kinds of books away from our children?"

Strong took another deep breath. Not only was this woman saying the cause of his organization was no longer important. She was suggesting that she might support others competing against LifeWatch for donations.

"Well, Beth Ann, not at this time. But I'll bring that up to the board to see if they have any interest."

They looked to the valet stand to see her husband tipping the attendant and climbing into the driver's seat of a new Mercedes. Once inside, he flashed his lights twice.

"Oh, that's my signal," Beth Ann said. "Thank you, again, for all you do, Dr. Strong. Y'all have a good evening." She clicked away in her high-heeled shoes to the passenger door, which was being held open by the attendant.

There seemed to be a void following Beth Ann Bridges's departure from the conversation. The two men stood beneath the portico a little longer. The uninformed passersby would assume that a famous, deeply respected gentleman was having a nice chat with an employee. The uninformed would be wrong.

Gaines looked deeply troubled.

"Is there something else, Tom?" Strong asked.

"We've had an unexpected turn of events, sir."

"What kind of unexpected turn of events?"

"Something happened this afternoon in Atlanta."

"Atlanta?" Strong felt an undeniable sense of dread in his gut. He'd feared this day would come.

"A medical facility there was destroyed—the one owned by Congressman Carlisle's son."

"What do you mean, 'destroyed'?"

"Someone detonated explosive charges at strategic points throughout the facility."

"No one suspects our organization, do they?" Tom was silent, but his silence spoke volumes. "Tom?"

"As you know, we had a man in that organization. You requested it several months ago when we learned they were experimenting with fetal tissue."

Strong thought back to a call he had received from one of LifeWatch's best donors over a year ago. The caller introduced himself as the founder of a patriotic organization in the Midwest and recommended Strong consider hiring a security professional named Sheffield. The man had military experience and in-depth knowledge of firearms, surveillance, and explosives. The caller was very convincing, and his organization's donations far surpassed whatever LifeWatch paid security professionals, so the hire was a no-brainer.

Six months after his hiring, Strong suggested Sheffield work his way into the Inc.Ubator organization, primarily as Strong's eyes and ears in an organization that could impact LifeWatch's success. Gaines agreed and reassured Strong that he would keep abreast of Sheffield's findings.

Only recently had media reports surfaced that the organization that recommended Sheffield was a radical paramilitary group with a violent past. Several of its leaders were under investigation for their radical efforts to bribe state and federal leaders. Gaines had reassured Strong that he would keep a close watch on Sheffield to ensure that LifeWatch wasn't implicated in anything illegal.

"Did you order the destruction of the clinic?" Strong asked Gaines.

Tom shook his head, no.

"Did this individual understand the directives?"

"Yes, he did. I'm sure of it."

Strong believed him.

"But I am afraid he took matters into his own hands, and things escalated."

"How could that happen?"

For the first time, Tom glanced away, but only briefly. "Weaker troops sometimes go rogue."

"Rogue! Goddamn it, Tom. We pay for the best hiring assessments, the finest communication devices, and a pretty good chunk of money for your ass, and you tell me this lone individual took matters into his own hands without your intervention?"

Gaines cleared his throat. "We're beginning to believe he was groomed for such a task by the people who recommended him."

Strong felt himself backed into a corner without options. It was all he could do to keep himself from punching the nearest face he could find, which in this case was that of Tom Gaines. "So what now?"

Tom said, "I promise you, sir, we will rectify the situation."

"You'd damn well better. I want a verbal report of your damage control plans the first thing in the morning. Is that clear?"

"Crystal."

"I thought we were going to find out what was going on in this clinic. Now I realize we may have ruined everything."

"Yes, sir." He waited in silence as the CEO of LifeWatch walked to the valet stand to retrieve his car. "By the way, sir. Dr. Dan Carlisle and several of his staff perished in the explosion."

"They got what they deserved," Strong muttered. He settled into the luxurious comfort of the BMW bucket seat and jerked the car into gear. As he sped away, he allowed the recent conversation, the current problems, to fade into the background so he could bask in one of his favorite pleasures.

His father had never had a car as nice as this one. In fact, no one in his lower-class family owned cars like this. For Strong, this car and the other trappings of his success were a part of his grand destiny. He had earned the acclaim, luxuries, and prestige he had attained. This recent "unexpected turn of events" was not going to stop him.

The BMW slipped through quiet back streets bordered with million-dollar mansions. Strong vowed to press on, no matter what got in his way. He would use this minor setback to propel himself forward. Now, he would have greater reach. He would be able to do more for his community and his nation.

He breathed in the sweet smell of success. Things would come together for him. He felt good. No, he felt great. He could hardly contain himself.

He chuckled.

It was time, after all.

In the dark parking lot, nestled next to a thick hedge, a Toyota Prius had sat idle during most of the evening's activities. Keith Edwards hunkered down behind the wheel and watched the two men chatting from across the parking lot. Keith assumed they were talking about how well Strong's performance had been received by the uninformed crowd at the banquet. Keith was not one of the uninformed. He was very informed, indeed.

As an accountant at LifeWatch, he knew donation levels were dismal. He'd seen the trends since the Supreme Court decision was leaked last spring. He knew how Joseph Strong would spin this and that his next steps would not be good. Strong would see the drop in giving as proof that his followers felt the battle had been won and that they no longer need to fight for this cause. In response, he'd ramp up calls for even stricter regulations and target liberal states more pointedly.

But Keith knew the response wasn't because people sensed victory. No, they felt guilty. They knew rights, whether they believed in them or not, had been taken away, and they were distancing themselves from organizations like LifeWatch. The parking lot before him was all the proof he needed. At other events like this, the lot would have been packed. Tonight, two-thirds of the spaces were vacant.

He ran stubby fingers through blond hair, noted the time on his watch, and jotted some comments in a notebook he had purchased from an office supply store. He could have lifted a notebook from the accounting department supply closet at the LifeWatch headquarters, but he wasn't the kind of man to steal office supplies from his employer. His notes on the LifeWatch banquet would go into a file folder, also purchased at the office supply store, and into a special box at his house.

When Strong drove away in his BMW, Keith started his Prius and slid through the parking lot. He followed the BMW from a distance until he was certain it was homeward bound. Then he slipped into a subdivision entrance, turned around, and headed home.

His mother's cat was purring and rubbing against his leg.

Allan hated that cat. It never wanted affection, except when Allan didn't want anything to do with it. It would sneak into Allan's room while he was away at school and pee on his bookshelf. Allan would come home to the most acrid smell floating from his bedroom. That cat had ruined many books with his powerful cat pee. No matter what Allan threw out or what he cleaned, he always smelled cat pee before falling asleep at night.

It must have just ruined some more books because the odor was back. The cat purred again and rubbed against Allan's leg. He opened his eyes, expecting to see familiar bedroom surroundings, but instead found himself lying on the kitchen floor in his own vomit. He wondered how the cat had gotten into his house.

He felt the rubbing against his leg again and realized it was the vibration of his phone. Aunt Julia was sending a text.

Dazed, he pulled the phone from his pocket and focused on the screen.

Get Out Now! the message screamed.

He pulled himself up by the kitchen counter and came face to face with several plastic buckets filled with tiny pellets. The ammonia smell—mixed with something else, maybe kerosene—made his nose burn.

He stumbled through the dark kitchen and into the living room as fast as he could, tripping over a footstool. He grabbed the backpack sitting in his bedroom doorway and staggered inside.

Gagging back bile to keep from throwing up again, he rushed into the bathroom and leaned over the sink. Just then, his phone vibrated again. He held it up to his face and read Aunt Julia's words. *MOVE IT! NOW!!!*

"All right," he mumbled to her, to no one, to himself. He turned and headed to the bedroom window, jerked it open, pushed through the screen, and had just started crawling out when the bomb went off. The impact propelled him through the window, along with half of the bedroom furniture. He crawled away from the exploding house as quickly as he could.

The roof over the kitchen shattered into thousands of pieces and shot into the sky, followed by the garage. Flames and smoke filled the night air.

He crawled into the neighbor's yard and behind a stand of cedars. More explosions rocked the night. Voices echoed here and there, as his neighbors ran out into the street to watch his house explode and burn. Someone stretched a garden hose as far as it would go and sprayed his front lawn.

The fire trucks arrived faster than he had expected. Within no time, they had taken over his neighbor's job and were spraying water on the house.

As Allan watched, a patrol car pulled up behind the fire trucks, lights flashing. Two police officers exited the vehicle and began to move the crowd back, away from the house.

Allan started to approach the policemen to request help when the bald man stepped out of the crowd and began to talk with one of the officers. It was obvious that the men knew each other. They shook hands and started what looked like an informal conversation.

Allan slipped back behind the cedars, hoping no one in the crowd had noticed him. Drugged, wounded, and dizzy, he somehow managed to crawl through his neighbor's backyard and into another neighbor's yard. Eventually, he stood up and jogged away from his burning house, the loud noises, and the police.

This time, he was more cautious. He stayed far away from lights and noises. He feared the bald man with the broken nose and eagle tattoo.

An hour later, he stumbled into the bathroom of a gas station. He used up most of their paper towels wiping the dirt, smoke, and smudges from his body. The gas station had Georgia Bulldogs sweatshirts on sale on a shelf in the back of the building, so he bought one and threw away his old shirt, which was stained with his own vomit. To shake off some of the effects of the drug he must have been slipped earlier, he also bought an energy drink and a couple of slices of pizza.

The earlier events left him with a dreaded sense of paranoia, so he felt it imperative to be as anonymous and untraceable as possible. Even requesting an Uber or Lyft might alert a savvy foe to his presence. He waited in the shadows near the gas station until a taxi neared. Stepping out into the open, he hailed the cab.

He had to get away. Away from the bald man, the flames, and his home.

The cab sped through the busy downtown area, where shoppers and diners strolled along the sidewalks like marines on a mission—very focused. One attractive woman, slender and wearing a brown poncho to shield herself against the evening chill, caught his eye. For a moment, she looked like someone from long ago. The person that she looked like wasn't a lost memory. In fact, he thought of her often, even after several years.

Her name was Amanda.

Allan had met her in a little café just off campus his first year of seminary. They dated for several months, and Allan felt he'd found the girl of his dreams.

Then, almost overnight, Dan Carlisle had come along and swept her, and Allan's dreams, away.

The lovely young couple moved on, leaving Allan and his hopes behind. The three got together from time to time, at campus events or political parties, but Amanda never looked back.

Until six months later when the phone awakened him in the middle of the night.

"Allan," a tearful voice pleaded through the darkness. "I need to talk to someone. Please. Can you come over?"

He leapt out of bed, dragged on the previous day's jeans and sweater, and headed for the door. Grabbing the pager Aunt Julia had given him when he entered seminary, he realized he had missed a page from her sometime during the night. He had been too busy, too tired lately. The page said, *Someone needs you!*

"Thank you for coming," Amanda said looking down at the doormat after he stepped through her front door. She wore a thick, white bathrobe over her nightgown. The image stirred feelings deep inside him. "I feel so bad about bothering you at this time of night." She handed him a cup of black coffee—a thank-you gift. "You still drink it black, right?" Her brown eyes sought his over the rim of the cup.

"Amanda, what happened?"

She moved into the living room of her small apartment, and he followed. They sat on the sofa, and she remained quiet, as if trying to gather the words they both knew she had accumulated even before calling him. "I've been going crazy," she began. "I needed someone to talk to, and you are the best listener I've ever known."

He appreciated the compliment, but he was missing his sleep. "Allan, I don't know what to do." He waited.

She parted her beautiful lips to speak, then stopped, and then started again. "I'm pregnant." She searched his eyes for a response.

"Are you sure?" That was the pat response all guys asked after hearing a woman was pregnant. Dumb and insensitive, but it just came out.

She nodded.

"Have you talked with Dan?"

She nodded again.

"And ..."

"He's turned away. He doesn't want anything to do with this."

Allan stared at the little patterns in the carpet. They reminded him of ripples in the sand at the beach.

"Dan is working overtime at the hospital. His classes are demanding more and more of his time. He doesn't have any energy to deal with a pregnant girlfriend." Allan imagined Dan using those very words to describe his feelings to her.

He breathed a deep sigh. In his soul he sensed they had reached one of those points in life in which everything changes. From this moment forward, nothing would ever be the same for Amanda, and maybe for Dan and himself, as well. This conversation, this event, this moment was pivotal. They were at a crossroads, and the outcome of their conversation would change the direction of their world forever.

"Tell me," he said.

"His father is beginning his reelection campaign. Rushing into a marriage or having a baby out of wedlock would devastate Congressman Carlisle's chances of getting elected. It would kill his mother." Tears cascaded down her cheeks. "I thought we'd been careful. I thought it was safe." Her hands were trembling.

He put his arm around her, and she melted into him. Sobs rose from inside of her, loud, uncontrollable. Allan let her cry.

"What can I do, Allan?" she pleaded.

He took another deep breath. As a seminarian, he knew the emotional gravity of the subject and both sides of the issue. He knew the devastation any decision would bring. In late night arguments and classroom debates, he had explored the options and found none of them to be close to ideal. He knew the decision had to be hers. He couldn't make it for her. But he was also aware that she was in such a state of shock, she could not think clearly. He reverted to counselor mode. "What are your options?"

"Oh, my God," she said. "I've covered these over and over in my head for hours. My best friend says I should have the baby, but that would kill my parents. They would be so disappointed. Besides, if word got out to anyone in the media, it would ruin James Carlisle's election hopes. Oh, I don't know, I don't know."

"That's one option," he said.

"I could have an abortion," she said, speaking the words in robotic monotone. "There are clinics in Atlanta. No one would have to know." In a moment, as if struck by a tidal wave, her expression went from controlled and steady to overwhelming grief. She burst into loud sobbing again. "I don't want to do that. I don't want that."

Allan held her again as she sobbed. She was shaking all over.

"Amanda," he whispered after a few minutes. "You have another option."

As if afraid of entertaining any other ideas, she raised her head and searched his eyes. "Another option?"

"Yes. You could marry me."

Her face brightened like a sunrise. Slowly, carefully, a smile came upon her lips. Then, just as carefully, a shadow crept over her face. She closed her eyes and shook her head. "It wouldn't work, Allan. I wish it would, but it wouldn't work."

"Think about it," he said. "We get along well. I enjoyed getting to know you before you met Dan. We could plan a quick wedding, and I could finish seminary."

"No," she said. "It's not my life. And you wouldn't want to raise someone else's baby, would you?"

"Sure I would. People do it all the time. Thousands of babies are adopted every year."

"But studies show children who are adopted tend to have more mental health issues. I wouldn't want to subject my baby to that."

"Amanda, the adopted children who are most at risk are those exposed to substance abuse, neglect, poor nutrition ... the two of us would not have those issues. Sure, there would be unusual challenges, but we are equipped to manage those challenges."

She paused, taking in the information. "No." She looked firmly into his eyes. "But it's so sweet of you to offer."

He felt defeated. He felt hopeless. As the problem solver, the guy who always found alternatives, he was out of ideas.

They had sat there for over an hour, not moving, not speaking. Allan thought long and hard, until his mind floated into numbness. He had never felt so hopeless and so helpless in his life.

THREE

In the back seat of that taxi, heading through Atlanta, Allan realized how alone he was. He had no one he could run to for protection. He glanced in the rearview mirror and, for a second, thought he recognized someone else sitting in the backseat. But looking closer, he realized it was just a play of the shadows and dancing streetlights illuminating his own image. But the likeness did remind him of someone who might help. Allan hadn't thought of him in years. He searched on his phone and gave the driver the address of a little run-down church on the south side of town.

Asbury United Methodist Church had once been the hub of activity in this part of Atlanta. On this evening, it was as quiet as the proverbial church mouse. Allan welcomed that silence as he welcomed the darkness. Both made him feel invisible and more secure.

Even in the darkness, he could see that the church needed a fresh coat of paint. The steeple, once a tall and impressive beacon to lost souls throughout Atlanta's south side, now seemed short and impotent. Deep ruts, patches of grass, and potholes were scattered throughout the once well-kept parking lot.

Standing at the base of the church, he realized that there had been a time when this would have been his destiny. While all young seminarians dreamt of leading a vibrant, growing church, the truth was, most of them would serve in churches like this before they pastored the larger churches of their dreams, if they ever did. These churches, with their declining member-ships, high debts, and decrepit facilities, were more often the norm for the inexperienced pastor with just a few years under his robe.

He studied the welcome sign in front of the church. His name could have been beneath the name of the church. Instead, it read, "Rev. Wesley Blake." Wes had been a good friend at Emory. Some people had even said the two seminarians looked alike. Allan assumed that was true, although he gave it little thought. Some professors even mixed them up, at least at the beginning of terms.

In older churches, the congregation often constructed a home or parson-age on church property for the minister and his family. That way, he could keep an eye on the church, both as caretaker and shepherd of the flock. In addition, the church congregation could always keep an eye on their pastor.

Asbury's parsonage needed almost as much repair as the church itself. Climbing the three steps to the front porch, Allan rapped on the screen door and backed down the steps. A harsh yellow light flashed on, illuminating the screened-in area. The front door opened, and a familiar, if aging, face appeared in the doorway.

"Yes," Wesley called. "May I help you?"

Even though he ached all over, Allan couldn't resist a chance to tease his old friend. "I'm looking for a place to stay for the night," he said.

"We support the homeless shelter over on Old Jonesboro Road," Wes called out. "They probably have room for you there." He started to close the door.

"Wesley, it's me, Allan."

"Allan?" He squinted into the darkness to try to recognize the man. "Allan Chappel?"

"Let me in, Wes," he said. "I need your help."

Wesley threw open the door, leapt down the porch stairs, and embraced Allan in a bear hug.

Allan screamed in pain.

"What happened?" Wes wrapped an arm around Allan's shoulder and helped him stumble inside the parsonage.

"It's a long story."

"This is incredible. You went to interview for a job, and somebody blew up the office?" Wes asked. "You might want to stick to your current job."

"Sounds unbelievable, I know."

"But that's not all," Wes continued. "A big, bald man with a broken nose chased you down and tried to kill you, right? Twice?"

Put so succinctly and devoid of the actual background, it sounded implausible. "Wes, how else would you explain these wounds?" Allan pointed to the scrapes they had bandaged with some gauze and tape Wes had found in his medicine cabinet.

"Man, you may have gotten hit by a car, mugged by some thugs, or you may have fallen out of bed this morning. I don't know. It just sounds too crazy to believe."

Allan melted into the old sofa, exhausted and worn. The pain was coming in waves, and he was tired of fighting it. "If you'll just let me crash here tonight, I'll go to the police in the morning."

"What about the bald man?"

"It'll be safer in the daylight. I just need to get to Inspector Johnson's office. Then I'll be all right."

"Okay."

It was getting late. Wes brought a pillow and some blankets from a closet and set them on the sofa beside Allan.

Allan looked around the shabby living room. Wes had once had such grand plans. He was going to build a mega-church, a church that would rival the biggest in the nation. But here he was, pastoring a little aging congregation on the south side of Atlanta. By his earlier standards, you could say he was going nowhere, but it looked like he had arrived.

"How's your church?" It was a question all ministers asked each other. Often, they answered with lies about attendance, radical programs, huge staffs, and mega-budgets. But the good ones took a humbler approach.

"We've got some good people. It may be falling apart, but I wouldn't want to be anywhere else," Wes said, and Allan sensed real honesty in his answer.

"I went through a divorce last year," Wes confessed. "Becky got the kids and most of the savings. I didn't have anything."

"God, that's tough." Allan studied his friend's face and was reminded of how many times he had been told that he looked like Wes. That was before the scrapes and bruises he'd received tonight.

"Hardest thing I've ever gone through." He looked up. "You know, ministers aren't supposed to get divorced." He looked back down to the aging carpet. "But sometimes it happens."

Allan didn't know what to say. "You're only human, Wes."

"Not to some…" Wes said, as if wanting to defend himself. His voice trailed off mid-sentence. "The church I was in didn't take it very well. Becky had some close friends there. Others were hung up on the whole divorce thing. So in June, I moved here."

Allan knew that some sins that were forgivable for church members were unforgivable for pastors.

"Asbury welcomed me, took me in, and nursed me back to health," he continued. "I know they've ministered more to me than I have to them, at least so far."

"That's great," Allan said, but his words sounded hollow. He wished he could say something more reassuring. He wanted to somehow support Wes but had nothing to offer.

"It's just a small congregation, mixed races, blue collar workers. I've performed more funerals this year than baptisms. But they've been very good to me." His blue eyes sparkled like streetlights on a foggy day.

They reveled in the late-night candor, and it reminded Allan of times long ago, sharing beliefs, philosophies, and bullshit in dorm rooms and one-room apartments during seminary. It made him miss those times.

"Let me show you my hobby," Wes said, looking up.

"Ministers aren't supposed to have hobbies," Allan joked. "Don't you know that they're supposed to work twenty-four-seven, three hundred and sixty-five?"

"Everybody needs a hobby. Hobbies keep you from working twenty-four-seven, three hundred and sixty-five, and that keeps you sane."

They went to the study, and Wes reached inside and switched on the light. The desk, books, and research items lined two of the walls in the room. In one corner, a small table held two DAT recording decks and a CD recorder.

A small audio mixer was at the front of the table. Several microphones on stands stood to one side.

"It's my own portable recording studio," Wes said. "It's not much, but I have fun with it. I've put most of my earnings into this, and I'm pretty proud."

"I never knew you were an audiophile," Allan said.

"It's just something I tinker around with a bit. Some guys rebuild old cars. Some surf the net. I record stuff."

"So, how's it work?"

"I can take this portable deck into the sanctuary and get a pretty good digital copy of our church choir. I can also take it into the city for street interviews. I edit material back and forth through the mixer," he said, placing a hand on the edge of the big flat device covered with control knobs. "And I can even burn CDs over here."

He inserted a tape into one of the DAT drives, and the beautiful sounds of a gospel choir filled the room through a pair of Bose speakers mounted in the upper corners. The music was almost perfect. Allan watched Wes drink in the sound, rocking a little back and forth to the rhythm. After a few seconds he stopped and said, "We have this young lady in the church who has one of the most beautiful blues voices I've ever heard, outside of professional blues bands." He took the first tape out of the deck and replaced it with another.

A rich and powerful voice floated through the speakers. "Sweet little Jesus boy. They made you be born in a manger. Sweet little Holy child. Didn't know who you were."

Allan felt deep chills down his back as the sound drifted throughout the room. He was speechless. He felt a sadness that started way down in his chest and swelled up to his throat, clenching it shut so he couldn't speak. Then, the sadness filled his eyes, and he felt them begin to overflow with tears.

After a few minutes of some of the most magnificent music Allan had ever heard, Wes reached over and switched off the deck. They both stood in silence, welcoming the emptiness, like someone who has just dined on a decadently rich dinner might welcome a break before dessert.

Somehow, the music made Allan feel closer to Wes. He now knew a side of his friend he had never seen before, and they both were better for it.

Allan broke the silence. "Would you mind if we checked out the eleven o'clock news?" He placed a firm hand on Wes's shoulder and coaxed him back toward the living room.

Wes switched on the small television in one corner and adjusted the channel to a local station. A couple of newscasters were giving teasers about upcoming reports.

"But first, we go to our on-the-scene reporter, Brad Kingston, for more on that abortion clinic bombing near Buckhead. Brad?"

The image of a young reporter standing before some burning rubbish appeared. "I'm here in front of an abortion clinic that was destroyed earlier today by a violent explosion. Police bomb-squad experts say multiple incendiary devices were detonated just a few hours ago. Shock tremors were felt up to half a mile away."

"It wasn't an abortion clinic," Allan said.

"TV news people don't lie," Wes countered, with a tinge of sarcasm.

"You're kidding, right?" Allan asked.

"Was anyone hurt in the blast, Brad?" the news anchor asked.

The street reporter looked down at a sheet of paper. "I'm told there were six people killed. No one who was in the building during the explosion escaped. Names are being withheld until the next of kin have been notified." Firefighters moved around in the darkness behind the reporter.

"That sounds horrible, Brad."

"Some are comparing this incident to the 1997 Atlanta abortion clinic bombing by Eric Rudolph." An image of Eric Rudolph appeared in one corner of the screen.

"Has anyone claimed responsibility for this bombing?" the newscaster asked.

"No single group has come forward as of this time," Brad said. "However, police are looking for a suspect who was taken to the hospital earlier this evening but slipped away unnoticed. The suspect's name is Allan Chappel."

A sketch that looked remarkably similar to Allan appeared on the screen, replacing Rudolph's picture. "This is an artist's rendition of Mr. Chappel, believed to be about six feet tall and in his mid-thirties. Police are asking anyone with news concerning his whereabouts to contact them."

The scene switched back to the news desk. One of the newscasters said,

"Anyone with information about this suspect is urged to call the Atlanta Police Department at 404-614-6544."

"Oh, shit," Allan muttered, sweat dampening his forehead. "Now I'm a fugitive."

"And I'm harboring you." Wes turned the volume down on the remote. "Is there anything you should tell me, Allan?"

He shook his head. "I went there for an interview, that's all. I think I was supposed to be in the building when they blew it up." At that moment, he wasn't sure if he was better off for missing the explosion.

"Who are 'they?'"

"I don't know. The bald guy. Somebody who wanted Dan to fail." Allan ran both hands through his brown hair. "I don't know what to believe. Maybe Dan's office was an abortion clinic, and he was going to share that part of it in our next meeting."

Everything seemed suspect. He wasn't sure of anything anymore, except the fact that the world had somehow gotten meaner. It seemed like everyone felt compelled to take any disagreement to the extreme. A simple, innocuous glance in traffic could turn to road rage in an instant. A questionable move in a child's sporting event could escalate to a major crisis. Walking or jogging through the wrong neighborhood could get you killed.

Allan had no idea what he had done to be targeted for death, but this bald man was relentless in his efforts. If only they could identify his motive, perhaps they could find a way to end the onslaught.

He sighed. Every breath felt heavy.

The friends sat motionless in the quiet, as the screen flashed images of talking geckos, sports cars, and tooth-brightening paste. Finally, Wes switched off the TV.

"Look, Wes. I don't know what I can say to convince you, but I'm not lying. I interviewed with this Inc.Ubator office. They were developing all sorts of medical breakthroughs, but they never said anything about performing abortions. At their request, I went to this psychiatrist's office. When I returned, the place was in flames. All right?"

"What about the bald guy?"

"All true. I swear." Allan raised his right hand to emphasize the truth, but the gesture felt silly and empty.

Wes shook his head. "I don't know what to believe. But I do know I'm tired and I need some rest. So do you. Get some sleep, and we'll talk in the morning."

He walked down the hallway to his bedroom. Allan heard the door close and the lock engage.

Allan turned off the lamp beside the sofa and stared at the ceiling. In one day, he had gone from hoping for an exciting new job to being a fugitive from the law who had dodged death twice. He'd started out owning a home and a car and now was lying on a borrowed couch in a friend's borrowed house. Incredible.

Carole Phillips snapped awake with a deep, painful feeling of dread. Something was wrong. Her first thoughts were of the project—had she missed an alert? Snatching up her phone, she scanned the screen for notifications, but none appeared.

She grabbed her bathrobe from the hook on the closet door and donned it while dashing down the stairs to her laboratory in the basement. Halfway down the steps she was reminded that the garment wasn't necessary. The community geothermal plant had provided plenty of heat for almost three decades—something independent-minded people back home would never believe was possible.

Pushing through the double doors, she was greeted with soft lights illuminating the molding near the ceiling and the low hum of fans cooling several laptop computers, which were placed side-by-side on a table running the length of one wall. She tapped the keyboard of the nearest computer and scanned the screen. All was normal . . . well, as normal as could be expected in a project like this.

The subject was functioning as expected. Heart rate was excellent. Blood oxygen level was within the normal range. The temperature was a degree higher than normal, but such fluctuation was common.

Carole slid down into the office chair in front of the table. Everything was proceeding as expected. So why did she feel such dread?

She pulled the robe snug around her neckline, bunching the material with her hand, and headed upstairs to her apartment. The morning light was beginning to filter through the blinds as she filled a cup with fresh water and placed it in the microwave. When the timer sounded, she extracted the cup and poured in a packet of coffee. The stuff was more bitter than anything they had back home, but it was what the people drank here, and Carole had grown accustomed to its taste.

She set the cup on the counter, opened her laptop, and began to peruse the news. She was reaching for the cup again when the CNN headline startled her and the cup fell to the kitchen floor, shattering into pieces.

"ATLANTA ABORTION CLINIC BOMBED"

She froze, oblivious to the coffee staining her robe and dripping down the cabinet doors. The clinic, located in North Atlanta, was destroyed by what appeared to be several explosive devices. Everyone in the office at the time was killed, including the clinic director, Dr. Dan Carlisle.

Her hands began to shake. The news was beyond devastating. Dan Carlisle and Inc.Ubator were responsible for her work here. They funded her entire project. Everything she did was threatened. There may be other investors who would find their work interesting, but it would take time and effort to find them.

A chill ran through her body as she realized that if someone attacked the Inc.Ubator office, the same person may try to hunt her down, as well.

A low-level filter alert buzzed her phone and reminded her that she had vital responsibilities here and now. She quickly mopped up the mess from the coffee cup and went downstairs to change the filter.

Although he was physically exhausted, Allan's mind would not relax.

The threats and dangers of the day brought back related memories. On the night that Amanda had confessed she was pregnant, she had also made a request—one he would never forget.

As the morning sun had threatened to creep in through the shuttered blinds, she lifted her head from his chest. "Allan," she whispered. "Take me to bed."

Obediently, he rose from the sofa and carried her to the bedroom. He laid her on her double bed and started to turn to walk away when she reached up and wrapped her arms around his neck.

"Stay with me," she said.

He wasn't sure whether this was an offer to rekindle the fire of their past relationship or a strange way of saying thanks for being there, or something else. He sat beside her and allowed her to pull his face down to hers. They kissed passionately and tenderly, pulling each other's clothes off and stroking each other's bodies. Afterward they lay in each other's arms in a dreamy half-sleep for a brief eternity. Sex is a powerful communicator, but Allan couldn't discern what Amanda was trying to say. Was this her way of dealing with the guilt she felt for getting pregnant? Was she trying to somehow show gratitude for Allan's willingness to help? Was she trying to lead him on or coerce him to support him or to forgive her, which ministers were supposed to do? Perhaps all that, and much more. Amanda, caught up in an agonizingly difficult situation was coping as well as she possibly could.

As the room filled with near-morning light, Amanda sat up, pulled the sheets over her beautiful breasts, and said, "I need your help."

"Okay."

"I'm going to take care of my situation, but I need you to go with me."

He was confused and getting more so by the minute. "What?"

"It's what I need to do, right now," she said. "I'll find a clinic across town."

"But what about us? What about what we just did?" His head was spinning as if he were drunk.

"Allan, I appreciate all you've done for me, and I really needed you today. But this is something I need even more now."

"Do you know what you're asking yourself to do? Do you know what you're asking me to do?"

"I know."

"This will change everything. Neither of us will ever be the same again."

"I know. Allan, I still need you there with me. No one else would understand. I can't do this alone."

"I don't know if I can," he said. Seminarians didn't take women to abortion clinics.

"Promise me."

He stared into her eyes, brushing his fingers against her cheek.

"Promise me," she said again.

"I'll be there."

She leaned over and kissed him gently on the lips. "I'll make the arrangements. We'll go tomorrow or the next day. I'll call you with the details." She got up from the bed and went into the bathroom.

Within a few minutes, he heard the shower splashing. He rose from the bed, put on his clothes, and left for home, as confused as a Southern boy could possibly be.

That day and the next, during every quiet moment, Allan prayed that Amanda would change her troubled mind.

A couple of days later, he picked her up at her apartment. She wore no make-up, projecting a no-frills, utilitarian mood. She was cold. She said little as they drove across the city to the clinic on the west side. She had chosen that facility because it was far enough away that they could be anonymous. They left the radio off.

He parked behind the building and started to walk around to Amanda's side to open the door for her, but she had already exited the car. He found himself glancing around suspiciously, searching for a familiar face, as they walked around to the front of the clinic. The street was empty, except for a passing taxi. The only sound was the tap-tap of their shoes as they walked quickly.

The lobby was humble. Soothing music played, and magazines were laid out on end tables beside a couple of sofas. The lighting was soft. The carpet was earthy. The whole place had a seventies feel to it. This place, here, now, was one of the few places that Allan had never thought he would be.

Amanda approached the glass window, talked with the receptionist, and came back with a clipboard.

Allan leaned close to her and said, "Amanda, if you don't ..."

"No," she insisted. "Don't say it." He backed off.

They sat down, and she began to fill out the documents. Allan looked for something to read but couldn't find anything that interested him. He picked up a magazine and thumbed through it. After returning the clipboard to the window, Amanda came back to the sofa. She slid her hand in under his arm and wrapped her fingers around his hand. Tightly.

Neither spoke.

Shortly, the nurse called Amanda's name, and she obediently stood and walked through the door to the back of the clinic.

Allan surveyed the waiting room again, wondering what was happening on the other side of the clinic doors and how Amanda would handle it. Two other women came into the facility while he was waiting. One had a rough, streetwise look about her. She wore a tight, short skirt and low-cut blouse. The other, a bit older than the first, looked like a waitress, maybe simply seeking low-cost care. He had no idea if either was pregnant or was there for other purposes. Each was escorted through the waiting room door.

Eventually the nurse came back to talk with Allan. "Your friend is doing well. She's sleeping now but should be ready to go home in about an hour. You might want to go out for a cup of coffee and return after she's had a chance to rest."

"Thank you, ma'am. I'll wait here."

"Suit yourself," she said.

The waitress came through a few minutes later. Allan watched her out of the corner of his eye. She seemed calm and relaxed and exited through the front doors.

He turned his attention back to the stack of magazines before him. Two articles about common myths in women's illnesses, one article about the joys of running, three articles on how to meet the ideal man. One hour and fifteen minutes later, the nurse opened the door, and Amanda slowly walked into the waiting room. Allan dropped the magazine and went to embrace her. She didn't hug him back but just leaned against him.

"She's going to be very tired," the nurse said. "See that she gets lots of rest."

"I will," he said and directed Amanda toward the exit. The nurse walked with them to the large wooden door and pulled it open.

"Take care," the nurse said.

Allan pushed through the clinic door.

"Murderer!"

"Baby killer!"

The mob must have assembled while Amanda was in the operating room. About twenty-five people, almost all white men, stood across the street brandishing protest signs and ugly posters. They had started yelling the second the door to the clinic opened. The posters were horrible, depicting grotesque images of aborted fetuses and terrible sayings.

Amanda pushed her head into Allan's chest, and he wrapped his arms around her in a protective way. They hustled along the short sidewalk across the street from the shouting rabble, toward his Honda.

"You're going to Hell," someone shouted.

Allan placed Amanda in the front seat and ran around to the driver's side. Hurriedly, he cranked the engine and roared out of the parking lot, well aware of the angry people glaring at them as they drove away.

Amanda was hunched over in her seat, hugging her knees to her chest. "I'm sorry. I'm sorry. I'm sorry," she said again and again.

Allan reached over and placed a hand on her shoulder to comfort her any way he could. She didn't seem to notice his touch. She was sobbing and began to rock back and forth in her crouched position.

"Amanda. It's all right. We're far away from them now." Allan continued driving across town with his right hand resting on her shoulder. She seemed to ignore his words and touch, sobbing louder and louder.

By the time they pulled to a stop in her apartment parking lot, her words had somehow changed to "I am so evil. I am so evil."

He turned off the ignition, pulled her across the gearshift, and smothered her in his arms. "No. You're not evil. No, Amanda."

Eventually she gained control and quieted down. The sobbing stopped. She sat up straight, wiped her eyes with a crumpled tissue she had carried with her from the clinic, and opened the car door.

Allan opened his door and hurried around to the passenger side. But she had already climbed out of the car and was walking uneasily toward her apartment door. He caught up with her, wrapped his arm around her waist and assisted her. He took her purse, found her keys, and opened the front door. She staggered into the apartment and walked straight to the bathroom, where she knelt before the toilet and threw up.

Hurrying in to help her, he grabbed a washcloth from the sink and soaked it in cold water. He used the cloth to wipe her lips. She began to moan.

Allan tried to comfort her as well as he could, but she was out of control. "Come on, Amanda," he said. He pulled her up ungracefully by the armpits and pointed her toward the bedroom. She sat down on the bed and allowed him to remove her blouse. Lying back, she let him tug her slacks off and rolled over into the sheets. He pulled the covers around her, and she turned away, hugging her pillow tightly.

He stayed in her room for an hour, wiping her forehead with the damp washcloth. Eventually, she fell into a disturbed sleep. He could see her eyes moving behind her closed eyelids.

He quietly got up and went into the living room, where he remained for the rest of the day.

He was there when she awoke. Amanda somberly entered the living room late in the afternoon and said in a low monotone, "Allan, it's all right for you to go home. I'm okay."

He searched her eyes for reassurance, and she seemed to force a smile in return.

"You'll call me if you need to talk?" he asked.

"Yes, of course," she said. She leaned forward and kissed him on the lips. "Thank you."

As he climbed into the driver's seat, his pager went off. He glanced down at the LCD screen and saw the words, *That's What Friends Are For.*

On the ride home, the emotions of the morning caught up with him. By playing straight, keeping everything in check, and controlling himself so he could help Amanda, he had pushed every feeling he had away until that moment. The clinic, the mob, and the gravity of what had just happened rushed over him and consumed him, and he began to cry uncontrollably. He pulled to the side of the street, put the car in park, and wept for a full fifteen minutes.

Drained, he put the car in gear, pulled back into traffic and headed home.

FOUR

The two men met before sunrise in Strong's office. "Let me see if I've got this straight," Strong announced from behind his executive desk, which was adorned with trophies and plaques. When he made such announcements, he wasn't really seeking confirmation. He was rebuking his head of security. It was a tongue-lashing meant to humiliate and correct an infraction. Tom Gaines was not just being "called on the carpet." Strong was using this moment to "mop the floor" with Gaines.

"One of our employees—"

"Excuse me, sir. Former employees," Gaines interjected.

Strong was visibly irritated by the interruption. "A former employee took it upon himself to kill numerous people at an Atlanta business."

"Well, yes sir. I've come to realize he was not stable. He struggled with PTSD from deployments in Afghanistan and Iraq. He has recently demonstrated poor judgement and a hostile attitude—"

"Poor judgement! Hostile attitude!" Strong shouted, kicking back his chair and rising to a standing position. "I would say so. Blowing up a building and killing six people is pretty goddamn hostile."

Gaines's demeanor was unshakeable, but his eyes couldn't hide the fear in his heart.

"Do you know what will happen if the media ties him to us? We'll be done. And probably in prison, too." Strong sucked in a deep breath of air and eased back into his chair. "This incident, this unexpected turn of events—" He glared at Tom, who struggled to return the stare, making Strong doubt that he was up to this task. "It's not going to stop us. If anything, it will be the catalyst that propels us to the next level."

"Yes, sir," Tom Gaines said. He regained his military stare.

"What are your plans to stop him?"

"I've alerted all of my staff. If he approaches the building, we will take him into custody."

"Not enough. What else?" Strong tapped the tip of his pen on the glass top of his desk, waiting for more.

"We've initiated a GPS search for his equipment, and we're closely monitoring all data transactions. We may contract with an outside source to bring him in."

"Another outside source? Hell no," Strong shouted. "We don't need more independent contractors fucking this up even more than it already is."

"Yes, sir."

"Keep it all internal. Use your own men. But find him and stop him any way you can."

Tom was quiet and stared ahead.

"I will begin to distance myself—our organization—from the clinic bombing. As soon as the media hears of this, they will surely try to pin it on us. I'll get the word out before they have a chance."

"Sounds good, sir."

"All right, Tom," Strong said. "Keep me informed."

"Yes, sir." He stood to leave.

"And Tom ..."

The security officer turned around.

"No more unexpected turns of events."

The bald stalker chased Allan through the narrow hallways of an old, wood-frame house, waving a long knife that gleamed in the dim light. Then a clash of thunder woke Allan and jolted him upright on the old sofa.

A thunderstorm tore at the oak trees outside. Storms like this—loud, threatening, dangerous, knock-the-power-out-of-your-house-and-take-two-pine-trees-with-it storms—reminded him of Amanda. It had stormed like this the night she died.

As his eyes adjusted to the light, he sank back into the soft pillows of the old sofa and scanned the room. Several cardboard boxes marked "WES—LIVING ROOM" sat in one corner. Masking tape held each box closed tight. A crumpled lampshade covered the lamp beside the tiny television. A section of wallpaper curled away from the ceiling. A clock ticked somewhere back in the kitchen. Soft snoring sounds came from behind Wes's bedroom door. An old picture frame displaying a photo of two cute, elementary school-age girls adorned an otherwise empty wall. Allan knew his old friend was going through hell.

He also knew there was really little he could do to help Wes. But sometimes a little can be a lot. He recalled how he and Wes used to go to Waffle House after all-nighters spent cramming for Greek exams. Wes had always ordered eggs, sunny side up, with bacon, double helpings of bacon. Maybe Allan could do something, no matter how little.

By the time Wes stumbled out from his room, wearing a pale blue bathrobe and white socks, Allan was fully awake and had prepared a large breakfast of pancakes, eggs, and bacon. "It's the least I can do to thank you for your help," he said to his sleepy friend.

"What, by cooking my food?" Wes asked. Then he added, "That bacon does smell good." He grabbed a strip and chewed it while he pulled up a chair.

"My thanks," Allan said and laid a steaming plate at Wes's place. "Coffee?"

Wes accepted a cup and lowered himself into the chair. "I haven't had anyone cook for me since ..." He let the words hang in the air.

"Yeah, I remembered the old Waffle House days and how much you liked their bacon and eggs. I always preferred their waffles, but your kitchen lacks the equipment for a real Waffle House." Across from Wes, Allan set his own plate on the table. "Wes, I've made a decision. If you want me to go to the police, I will. I'll face the music and take my chances."

"Allan—" Wes started.

"No. Let me finish. I don't think they will believe me. You said it last night. It sounds crazy."

Wes nodded. "It really does, Allan. I'm still finding it hard to believe."

"Before I talk to the police, I need to find out why the bald guy targeted me. I need more information. I need to do some research."

"What kind of information?"

Allan caught himself rubbing the tattoo on his wrist—something he often did while thinking. "In our interview, Dan mentioned several consultants living in other parts of the country. If I can get hold of them, maybe we can find out why someone would try to destroy Dan's office and kill him."

"Fair enough. However, don't you think the guy who destroyed Dan's office would go after the others involved as well?"

Allan stabbed the air with his fork. "Yes, if he knows they exist and if he finds them first. Although, I'm not sure all of them had enough information about everything that went on there. Dan said they were each involved in different projects."

"How will you find them?"

Allan took a deep breath and struggled to choose the right words to get Wes's support. It was critical that Wes agree to help for this plan to work. "Part of the interview process included a visit with Dr. Chamberlain, a psychiatrist who had an office on Peachtree Street, to take tests and profiles. We must start with her. She's the only link to Carlisle I have who wasn't in the Inc.Ubator office when it blew up."

"Okay," Wes said. "We call Dr. Chamberlain. Then what?"

"Well, you call her," Allan said. "After all, I'm a wanted man."

"Wait," Wes protested. "Why would I call her?"

"Just make an appointment and get into her office."

"An appointment? For what?"

"Her receptionist keeps files in her desk drawer. She had a file on Dan's organization. I saw it. I need that file."

"Whoa! You want me to steal a file from her office? No way. I'm already in way over my head just talking with you."

Allan stood up, walked to the kitchen counter, and retrieved the coffeepot. He poured some of the black serum into Wes's cup and then his own. "This is the only way I can find out what I need to know to support my case," Allan said. "Besides, I'll steal the file. You just need to leave the door open."

"How's that?" Wes ran his fingers through his hair.

Allan stood behind his own chair and leaned forward, resting both hands on its back. "Yesterday, when I visited her, she mentioned her receptionist takes a lunch break every day at noon. If you can insist on a noon appointment, spend an hour in her office, and unlock that front door, I'll do the rest."

"But what if somebody sees you?

"If someone recognizes me, I'm just another fugitive. What else would you expect from me? I'll simply sneak in behind you and take a picture of the file from the receptionist's desk."

"I don't know..."

"Wes. I need that information. My life may depend on it." He forced eye contact with Wes and saw a glimmer of hope in his expression.

Wes caved for a moment. "All right. What do I need to do?"

Like a salesman who had just closed a big deal, Allan felt a rush of adrenaline. He started to pace the floor in front of the table, ready for action. "Just make a counseling appointment this morning. Insist on seeing her at twelve o'clock. Tell her you're feeling bad about your divorce, and that noon is the only break you have in your schedule. Then, once you're in the office, come out to the lobby at about twelve fifteen and unlock the front door. I'll slip inside after you've gone back into the office."

"How can I do that?"

"Tell her you've gotta pee," Allan said. "I don't know. Just unlock the front door and I'll take care of the rest." His insistence seemed to make Wes feel more uncomfortable, but getting the file was far more important than comfort.

"I don't know, Allan. What if her secretary doesn't go to lunch at noon, or I can't get out to unlock the door?"

"Then I owe you for the cost of one counseling session, and we're done," Allan countered.

"What if I can't get an appointment today at noon?"

"Then we'll have to come up with an alternative. I've gotta get that file, Wes."

Wes dabbed the runny egg yolk with a slice of toast and shook his head back and forth. Allan didn't think he would agree.

"All right," Wes said. "But after you get what you need, you disappear. Okay?"

"You'll never see me again, until this all blows over," Allan said. "Then, I'll join your church. I'll tithe. Your membership will increase."

Wes shook his head again. "Yeah, when I'm a prison chaplain."

———————————

Wes tried to talk his way out of the crime all the way to Dr. Chamberlain's office, but Allan was resolute.

Earlier that morning, Wes had called the counselor's office according to plan and made an appointment through Rachel, the receptionist. He'd explained that he was distraught over his divorce, had not slept in several nights, and needed to talk with someone. He mentioned several ministers on the north side of the city, saying they had worked with Dr. Chamberlain in the past. He also insisted on talking with Dr. Chamberlain at noon. It worked.

He dropped Allan off a couple of blocks away from the counselor's office building at 11:30 and drove on. Allan watched from afar as Wes entered the building through the front doors.

Allan waited by a MARTA bus stop and scouted the office structure. At twelve o'clock—right on time—Rachel walked out the front door. She entered a Honda in the parking lot and drove away.

Allan jaywalked across the street, scrutinizing all the people and cars he could see. He wiped a thin sheen of sweat from his forehead and hurried past the front door. He paused for a second to see if anyone might be following, then turned and entered the main lobby. He mounted the stairs to Dr. Chamberlain's office on the second floor. There, he slipped on a pair of surgical gloves he and Wes had purchased from a nearby pharmacy. The door was unlocked. He opened it as quietly as he could and stepped inside.

As he suspected, the outer office was empty. Behind Dr. Chamberlain's office door, he could hear Wes talking. A lot. It sounded like he was really putting on a good show. Allan moved closer.

"I really don't understand why she left me for someone like that." His voice sounded like he was crying. "I trusted her," he continued.

At that point, Allan realized Wes was not acting. He was really talking with his therapist about his painful divorce, and she was apparently helping him work through some deeply hidden trauma. Listening to his story was like watching bad pornography. Allan felt dirty and guilty.

He walked around the receptionist's desk and tried the file drawer. It was locked. Reaching into his jacket pocket, he retrieved a couple of screwdrivers, which he had lifted from Wes's garage. He'd known he might have to break the lock on the drawer to get to the files, but he hadn't let Wes in on this important piece of information.

He slid one of the screwdrivers into the slot between the desk and the drawer. It barely fit. Pulling the handle up, like a lever, he pried the drawer out of the cabinet. It opened with a loud crack.

Allan froze.

The doctor's office became silent. "Did you hear something?" Dr. Chamberlain asked.

Wes's voice got louder. "No, ma'am. I didn't hear anything. I was just saying I would have done anything, absolutely anything to make our marriage work. I didn't want a divorce. I didn't want to be away from my daughters. I didn't want any of this." He started to cry again.

Apparently, it worked because Dr. Chamberlain did not come into the lobby to check out the loud noise.

Allan found the folder marked Inc.Ubator and opened it on the receptionist's desk. Using his phone, he began to snap pictures of every page in the folder. It didn't take long. There were only fourteen pages inside.

After he finished, he returned the folder to the drawer and slid it shut. The extended locking mechanism prevented the drawer from closing. He inserted the screwdriver into the slot between the drawer and the desk once again and reversed the process he had used to open the drawer. The drawer slid in more easily this time.

He quietly walked through the lobby and slipped out the door.

At that point, he realized he had not thought of everything. Dr. Chamberlain would notice the unlocked door and become suspicious. He could not lock the door from the outside. Wes would have to manage by himself.

He slipped out the front door.

When Wes entered the coffee shop down the street from Dr. Chamberlain's office, Allan was already waiting for him with an extra-large cappuccino.

He noticed that Wes's eyes were swollen and red. "You okay, man?"

"Yeah. That was kinda tough."

"Well, know that I really appreciate your help. I owe you one."

"More than that, my friend."

"Look, Wes. I forgot about the front door. Did the doctor notice the unlocked door when you left?"

"Wasn't an issue. The receptionist, Rachel, returned from lunch before I left."

Allan said, "Rachel may say something to Dr. Chamberlain about that, and she might call you and ask questions."

"If she does, I'll tell her I must have left it unlocked when I went to the restroom," Wes said. "Besides, she won't have to call. I made a follow-up appointment for next week."

"Really?" Allan looked again into Wes's swollen eyes and realized the meeting had helped his friend, and not in a small way.

Wes looked down at the floor. "I guess I really needed that."

Allan nodded. "If she asks, just stick to your story. And deny knowing me."

"Yeah, all right," Wes said. Then, as if trying to lighten the mood, he added, "What was your name, again?"

They drove to Wes's house, and Allan printed the photos. He missed his own computer equipment. Allan couldn't afford much, but Wes's equipment was much shoddier than his. The pages were a hodgepodge of different information: a newspaper article by Dr. Collins at the University of Tennessee, a journal abstract about blood clotting written by a professor in Houston, and another abstract about the gestation time frames of different mammals. Others looked similar to documents Allan had seen in Dan's office.

Wes stopped studying a list of lab sites and pushed the page in front of Allan. "You said this morning you wanted a list of consultants. Is this what you're looking for?"

Consultant Locations

Dr. Jason Ayers	Atlanta, GA
Dr. Chris Collins	Knoxville, TN
Dr. Alfredo Griffin	Chicago, IL
Dr. William Smallwood	Houston, TX
Dr. Carole Phillips	Klaipeda, lt.

Looking at the paper, Allan said, "That's it! Dan showed me that in his office."

"I wonder what each one did for the Inc.Ubator organization," Wes said.

"We've got an article by Dr. Collins from University of Tennessee in here somewhere. Must be the same Collins," Allan said.

"I saw another article from Smallwood in Houston," Wes said.

Allan pushed Wes out of his chair and took his place, typing and clicking buttons. "Look! There's a Dr. Griffen at the University of Chicago."

Wes placed a check mark by Collins, Griffen, and Smallwood. "Maybe they can help us understand more about Inc.Ubator," Wes said.

"Let's see," Allan said, grabbing his cell phone. "You call Collins in Tennessee, and I'll try Griffen in Chicago. Ask if they have any connection with Dan Carlisle or this Inc.Ubator organization."

"But what if they do have a connection?"

"Ask them for more information about the purpose of the organization."

The somber room came alive with activity as the two searched for people who might provide clues to the truth about Inc.Ubator. Wes Googled Dr. Chris Collins in Knoxville, Tennessee. Before he could dial the number, Allan had reached the Griffen residence in Chicago.

"Hello. May I speak with Dr. Griffen?" he said. He looked up at Wes, sharing the anticipation of the moment.

Wes paused to hear the conversation.

"Yes, Dr. Griffen," Allan said. "Oh. I'm terribly sorry. I didn't know. No, I don't need the address. Thank you." He hung up his phone, stunned. A cold sweat peppered the back of his neck. "Oh, shit. Griffen died in an automobile accident three days ago. She said he lost control of his car and crashed."

Wes slowly dialed the number for Dr. Collins. The phone rang four times and went to voice mail. The generic message played, "Please leave a message at the tone."

"Hello, Dr. Collins," Wes said. "My name is Allan Chappel, and I am calling to talk with you about an organization here in Atlanta called 'Inc.Ubator.' I've been offered a position with this organization by Dan Carlisle and was given your name as one who might be able to provide some background information."

Allan nodded his head as if to indicate that the ruse sounded good.

Wes left Allan's phone number and hung up. He returned to scanning the contact list as Allan's phone rang.

"Who the fuck are you?" a young-sounding female voice demanded on the other end.

"Uh, I beg your pardon?"

"Dr. Collins has absolutely nothing to do with Dan Carlisle or Inc.Ubator, and we will have you arrested if you come near us," she said, her voice almost a shout.

"I didn't mean to—" Allan stuttered.

"I don't give a shit what you meant. Leave us alone," her voice trembled.

"I'm sorry to bother you."

The phone clicked off.

Allan looked at Wes. "Shit."

"Was she mad?" Wes asked.

"More scared than mad," Allan reflected.

"At least it sounds like he's still alive," Wes said. "Not like Dr. Griffen. Who's next?"

"I don't know. Dr. Carole Phillips, I think." Allan scrutinized the list.

"What state is 'lt'?"

Wes looked closer. "I don't have any idea. Could it be a typo?"

"I doubt it. They were pretty thorough." Allan leaned in closer. "You know, these letters are lower case."

Wes pulled the paper to his side of the table. "That's strange. Why would 'lt' be in lower case while all of the other states are in upper case?"

"It's not a state," Allan said. "'lt' is a country. What country uses the abbreviation 'lt'?"

He pulled the laptop to his side of the table and searched the internet. Wes grabbed an encyclopedia from a bookshelf.

"This is it!" Allan announced, gazing at his screen.

Wes stepped behind him.

"Lithuania—'lt' stands for Lithuania."

"Lithuania? As in the former Soviet Union?

"Oh, my God," Allan said, realization washing over him. "That's right. Dan said he wanted me to talk with Dr. Carole Phillips, but that it would be too late. I didn't understand what he meant by that at the time. I thought she was coming to work later. Now it's clear. I couldn't talk with her because she was in another time zone on another continent! Is Klaipeda in Lithuania?"

Wes scanned the encyclopedia page. "Klaipeda, the third largest city in Lithuania. They had a consultant in Klaipeda, Lithuania."

"But why?" Allan rubbed the tattoo on his wrist and started pacing. "If she's in Lithuania, there might be something else, some remnant of research still left somewhere. Search 'Klaipeda,' and see if there is any reference to Dr. Phillips." He pushed the laptop to Wes's side of the table. "'Phillips' doesn't sound like a Lithuanian name," Wes muttered while punching keys. "No. Nothing. Maybe that office is closed."

"Maybe," Allan said. "I'll try Google." His search for a Dr. Carole Phillips in Klaipeda, Lithuania came up empty. "Dead end," he said.

"Let me try Dr. Smallwood," Wes said. He found the number and dialed it. Allan waited while the phone rang.

"Hello?" Wes said. "I'm calling for Dr. Smallwood—Oh, my. I'm so sorry. Please excuse me. I'm sorry for your loss." He hung up the phone and quietly said, "Heart attack, day before yesterday. Oh, dear Lord. What have you gotten yourself into?"

Allan and Wes stared at each other. Wes's words hung between them. "So, we have one doctor missing, two dead, and one we can't reach in another country, right?"

"Plus, a bombed-out office with six dead bodies."

"Man, this is way over our heads."

Silence descended like a thick fog and filled the room. The clicking clock in the kitchen sounded like a giant metronome, tapping off the final beats of a death march.

Then Allan's phone buzzed in his pocket. Pulling it out, he knew that the warning text message from Aunt Julia was unnecessary.

You need to move on, the message said, obviously tapped hastily into her cell phone in Surprise, Arizona.

But Allan had already decided. He kicked the base of the old couch with his heel. "We don't have enough information."

"I don't know where you're going to get more," Wes said.

"I've gotta talk to Dr. Collins, in Knoxville."

"You think he knows more?"

"I don't know any other way to get more information."

"Yeah. You're right." Wes's dark eyebrows almost seemed knitted together in his deep thought. They reminded Allan of a comment Aunt Julia had once made when he was trying to be psychic, like her. He was just a boy, and she had come to visit them in Tampa. He had stared intently at her and felt his forehead wrinkle in desperation.

"Allan," she'd said, "you can't force the psychic powers. Either they come or they don't."

"But I want to be able to tell the future, like you," he'd replied.

"First, I don't tell the future. I simply sense the ebb and flow of our spirit forces."

"Okay. I want to sense the ebb and flow of our spirit forces."

"Rubbing your eyebrows together won't make that happen." She had lovingly cupped her palm around his ear and looked deeply into his eyes. "It has to just happen."

Allan looked closer at Wes's eyebrows. "I need a disguise," he said. "For years, you and I have been told we look alike. Dr. Jenkins used to get us confused all the time in Old Testament class. If I could dye my hair and cut it a bit, and . . ."

"What are you thinking?" Wes said, a tinge of hesitation in his voice. He stared at his old friend, waiting for him to ask the obvious. But Allan had asked too much of Wes already. He couldn't bring himself to do it.

Wes looked reluctant but said, "I'm not sure if you can pull this off, but you can take my driver's license and passport."

Allan exhaled a sigh of relief. "It's the only way I can find out who's behind this," Allan insisted.

"I just don't think you're that good looking," Wes said with a laugh.

That afternoon, Wes went to the local pharmacy to pick up some hair dye.

Allan sequestered himself in the tiny bathroom and rubbed the stuff into his hair. His hair was sandy brown, and Wes's was darker. But it didn't take much work to make the transition. He saved a bit to darken his eyebrows, and finally, while his hair was still wet, he clipped it until it was noticeably shorter.

Walking out of the bathroom, he approached Wes, who was sitting on the sofa in front of the small TV. Wes stared in astonishment. "You know, this might just work."

They sat together on the sofa, and Wes said, "Wow. I feel like I've found my long-lost twin brother." They both chuckled. "And, if you're wearing a face mask, you might just get away with this." He paused to change the subject. "Have you given any more thought to why they're chasing you?"

"I can't figure it out," Allan said.

"So, what do we know?" Wes raised his index finger. "First, we know that there were several consultants around the country and one in Lithuania who worked with Dan."

"Yeah, but we still don't know what Dan's company did or why someone killed him. The fact is this," Allan said, becoming irritated that he couldn't come up with a conclusive answer, on top of everything else that had happened. "For some reason, someone killed six people in that office and several others around the country, and he's trying to kill me."

"It seems obvious that they think you know more than you know, so you threaten them. If they get rid of you, they get rid of the threat," Wes added.

"Or maybe they kill two birds with one stone," Allan said. "They get rid of me, and they set me up as the fall guy." He froze. "Shit. That could be true." Allan turned as somber as the gloomy home in which he was hiding.

Wes spoke up. "We just won't let that happen. They'll have to find someone else to blame."

"Thanks, Wes," Allan said.

"I hope you find what you're looking for."

"Yeah. I feel like I'm running out of time."

When he came home, Strong had walked straight into the living room and switched on the television to watch the local news. Its luminescence glared and caused strange shadows to gather like demons in the corners of the room. He glanced at the clock on the screen and realized he had not moved from in front of the set since arriving home forty-five minutes ago.

He eased back into his recliner and held the remote in the air, continuing to change news channels, when his cell phone vibrated. Caller ID indicated that Paul Dwight, Chairman of the Board of LifeWatch, was calling.

"Joseph? Have you seen the news?"

"Yes, sir. I'm watching it right now."

"I'm concerned," Dwight continued. Dwight had recently gone through radiation therapy for throat cancer, and his voice sounded like it was full of small rocks. "The media will tie this bombing to groups like ours."

"I share your concern," Strong said.

"They can make you look pretty bad, you know. They'll hound you like a hunting dog. They'll scrutinize every politician and every political action group you've ever worked with to dig something up."

"They'll have to work very hard to spin this in our direction," Strong said. He noticed the fingers on his right hand were digging deeply into the leather arm of his recliner.

"Do they have any ground to stand on, Joseph?"

"None whatsoever. LifeWatch is as spotlessly clean as any organization can be. We never advocate for violence, in any situation, and we cannot be held accountable for the behavior of a few unbalanced individuals."

There was a pause on Dwight's end, as if he wanted more reassurance.

"Believe me, Paul. They will never connect the abortion clinic bombing to us."

"If they did, it would be devastating."

"Yes, it would. But it will not happen."

"Let me know what I can do to help," Dwight said.

"Right."

———————————————

Late in the afternoon, Wes drove Allan into downtown Atlanta.

Allan's phone chimed, announcing a text message from Aunt Julia.

Be Careful! the message read.

"Have I ever told you about my Aunt Julia?"

"No, not that I can remember."

Allan played with his phone while he talked. "Well, for starters, she's my favorite aunt—lives by herself in a town named Surprise in Arizona. The name fits."

Wes nodded.

Allan watched Wes out of the corner of his eye. "Aunt Julia's psychic."

Wes gulped a bit. "Psychic? Really?"

Allan nodded. "All my life she's said things that seemed to come true. She warned me about playing on an old, rotting playground swing, or about certain friends I had."

"And her warnings came true? They really happened?"

"No, not all of them. But enough to make me a reluctant believer."

"Allan, real psychics don't exist."

"I'm not so sure. Once, she told me; 'Stay away from the woods.' That weekend, I chose not to go on a scout camping trip. It rained cats and dogs, and every scout came home sick. Some of the kids stayed out of school for a week."

Wes frowned.

"I know this is hard to buy into. When I went to college, she turned techno. She gave me a fax machine and sent cryptic psychic faxes, every now and then. My junior year, I got one from Aunt Julia which said, *U2.* I rushed over to the Student Union and was able to get the best seats in the house for the U2 concert."

Wes held up a hand and shook his head. "That ain't proof."

"No, but it's an interesting coincidence," Allan said. "When I went to seminary, she sent me another gift—a pager. She started sending psychic pages instead of faxes."

"A psychic upgrade. That is wild," Wes said. "However, as a minister, I'm expected to denounce such evil practices as being 'of the devil.'" He wagged a finger in Allan's direction. The day's tensions seemed to make Wes act loopy.

Their friendship was now somehow tighter than it had been in seminary, and Allan felt compelled to tell a story he'd never told before. He took in a long, deep breath, let it out slowly and stared at the road ahead of them. "One night, I received one of Aunt Julia's psychic pages. It simply said, *Help! She needs you*, but I knew exactly who she was referring to."

Wes leaned forward.

"You never knew Amanda Taylor at Emory, did you?" Allan realized he was rubbing the tattoo on his wrist.

"No."

"Education major. I met her my first year of seminary and fell for her, hard."

"I'm surprised I never knew her."

"She was an undergrad. A couple of weeks after we started dating, she met Dan Carlisle and dumped me. I still had strong feelings for her. She and Dan and I ran into each other here and there, but that was about the extent of our friendship."

"So, your aunt's page?"

"When my pager went off, I knew instinctively that it was about Amanda. I went to her apartment, but the place was locked up. I knocked, but no one came to the door." He paused, recalling the vivid memory. "It was storming that night, and I was soaking wet."

"What did you do?"

"I went around back. She had a little patio with a glass door on the backside of her apartment. That door was also locked. I looked through the vertical blinds and could see someone lying motionless in the bathtub. I pounded on the door, but she didn't move. So, I grabbed a metal table on the patio, swung it around in a circle, and threw it through the glass."

"Jeez."

"She was wearing a white bathrobe that had turned red from the bloody water. When I pulled her from the tub, her body was cold and limp. I tried her pulse. I checked her breath. Her eyes were dim. I didn't know what to do." Allan's voice grew softer. Something tightened in his throat.

"Were you in time?"

Allan wiped his brow with his sleeve. He noticed Wes was sweating, too. "I saw an empty pill bottle on the floor and an empty wine bottle under the toilet. Her wrists were in shreds."

"Oh, my Lord."

He had replayed the scene in his mind a million times before, but it now came back with an emotional vengeance when he described it out loud. He couldn't stop the tears from raining down his cheeks. "I called nine one one and reported the emergency. The ambulance came in just a few minutes, but there wasn't anything the paramedics could do. They put these little foam pads on her body and tried CPR, but it was too late."

"Man, I am so sorry. I never knew..."

"The police asked me a bunch of questions. I didn't mention Dan Carlisle, 'cause I knew it would come back to haunt him and his father's re-election campaign."

"What do you think happened?" Wes asked. "I mean, why did she take her life?"

"I know exactly what happened," Allan said. "Carlisle got her pregnant. She panicked and had an abortion." Allan didn't mention how he knew, and Wes didn't ask.

"I found all these gruesome pamphlets from antiabortion groups around her bedroom. I think they made her feel guilty, and she couldn't take it. I never realized how vulnerable she was."

"Did Dan know?"

"Not till I told him. He was shocked, had no idea."

Wes seemed to dwell on this for a moment, as if trying to find the right words. "Isn't it strange that Dan contacted you, after all these years, to offer you a job with his new company?"

"Yeah. I've thought about that. He might have been seeking some sort of redemption or reconciliation by reaching out to me. After all, I found her, and I covered for him."

"People respond to guilt in strange ways," Wes said.

"Yeah."

Wes remained quiet once again, and the car became almost confiningly silent. Then he asked, "Allan, is that why you dropped out of the ministry?"

Fatigue, stress, and memories from years ago overcame Allan. Great tears rolled down his cheeks again. He nodded and wiped his sleeve across his nose. "That was a big part of it."

FIVE

Carole paced in her small living room like a prisoner on death row, which seemed appropriate, based on the reports she had read from Atlanta. She couldn't reach Dr. Carlisle, or anyone else in the Inc.Ubator organization, for that matter. She fought the ever-present urge to run. There was no way she could leave the project for ten or twelve days, and there was no one she could leave it with.

The papers had accused someone named Allan Chappel of destroying the Inc.Ubator offices in Atlanta. Carole couldn't imagine why he would do such a thing. In her mind, the process Dan's Carlisle's team had developed offered so much promise, so much hope. It wasn't perfect, but nothing is, and it was better in some situations for some people.

Carole straightened up the living room a bit and headed downstairs for her morning monitoring session. She wondered if the current circumstances could change everything. Was it fair—no, was it cruel—to continue the process if the entire system was about to end?

She was so close. Less than two weeks, and she could safely shut everything down. She had to continue, no matter what. She could deal with the fallout later.

Wes pulled into the parking lot of the Greyhound station where Allan caught a bus for Chattanooga, Tennessee.

On board the bus, Allan inspected the contents of a backpack that Wes had given him when they left his house. Wes had stuffed the copies of the files they had stolen from Dr. Chamberlain's office in the front pocket. At the bottom of the pack was his wallet. Allan found a couple of hundred dollars inside along with Wes's driver's license and credit card. In addition, his friend's passport was beneath the wallet. A sticky note inside said, "With your new hair color, this might help you go wherever you need to go. I believe in you. Wes."

Late that night, the bus stopped in Chattanooga where Allan waited for another Greyhound bound for Knoxville, Tennessee. Allan's eyes caught a television in one corner of the bus station as he waited and dampness chilled the back of his neck. His hand-drawn likeness, before the new haircut and coloring, flashed on the monitor. The CNN ticker running along the bottom of the silent screen proclaimed authorities were searching for the man in the drawing in connection to the recent abortion clinic bombing in Buckhead, a northern Atlanta suburb.

Allan absentmindedly rubbed his right wrist with his left thumb. Looking down at the dark blue tattoo, displaying the name "Amanda," across his wrist, he realized that the inspector had seen that tattoo. It could be used to identify him. He tugged a shirtsleeve over the blemish to hide it.

He didn't have much time. Scanning the room, he searched for knowing looks among the other occupants of the bus station, but no one appeared to notice. They were all wrapped up in the dull oblivion of typical passengers.

He boarded the next bus, where he leaned against the window and feigned sleep. Eventually, the other passengers joined him, and the bus rambled away toward Knoxville.

SIX

Knoxville, a sleepy city nestled in the Great Smoky Mountains, had been home to one of the last world's fairs in 1982 and still proudly displayed many of the structures that had been constructed for that event.

But Allan arrived in Knoxville with no plans for sightseeing. He needed to discover what had happened to the Inc.Ubator consultant there.

He had spent the night snoozing on the bus and on a bench in the Knoxville Greyhound station. In between uncomfortable naps, he'd studied the files again. He reread the newspaper article about Dr. Chris Collins, a UT professor and strong advocate for stem cell research. If anyone in Knoxville could help him, Dr. Collins could.

UT's campus stretched through much of the downtown area. Allan checked campus directories, made a phone call to the academic dean's office, and found Dr. Collins's office location. The doctor wasn't in, but the class schedule was posted on the office door.

He grabbed a latte and a muffin at a campus cafe and waited for the ten o'clock class to begin.

Students pushed their way into the large auditorium and took their seats around the theater. Some talked loudly in small groups, here and there. One boy tossed a football across the room to a friend on the other side.

A young woman was preparing handouts at the front of the class, so Allan approached her. She was dressed casually in jeans and a sweater, which fit snugly around her large frame.

"Excuse me," he said.

She seemed impatient as she sorted the handouts into stacks. "Yes?"

"I'm thinking about attending grad school at UT, and one of my professors insisted I attend a lecture by Dr. Collins. Can I attend this lecture?"

She looked up from her stack and scrutinized him closely. He felt like he must have passed the test. "Dr. Collins won't be in class today," she said. "I'm the teaching assistant, and I will deliver the lecture. I'm Jennifer Thompson," she said, extending her hand.

Allan did not offer his name. "Nice to meet you. I know you must be busy," he said, searching for a way to find more information about the doctor's whereabouts. "Will he be in his office later today? I was hoping to talk with him."

A knowing look passed over her face. "Dr. Collins is out of the office all day. I'll be glad to mention you were here," she said. "What is your name?"

"Allan Chappel," he said.

She stepped back as if she was now leery of any contact. "Mr. Chappel, Dr. Collins does not want to talk with you. I made that clear on the phone a couple of days ago. Stay the fuck away from us." She returned to her paper sorting.

Her words stung like a thorn. "Look, Ms. Thomas," he said. "My life is in danger, and Dr. Collins may be in danger, too. I may be able to help you protect him."

She glared. "You really don't know anything, do you. The best protection is to keep away from back-jobs like you."

Allan slunk out the door, jilted and rejected, as Jennifer quieted the class and began the lecture. In the last three days, he'd survived two bomb blasts, a tumble into oncoming Atlanta traffic, and a couple of police chases. But this last blow was the icing on the cake.

Allan paced back and forth in the lobby for an hour and a half as Jennifer Thomas lectured the class.

When the students scrambled out, heading to dorm rooms, the library, coffee shops, or keg parties, Allan slipped back into the auditorium in time to see the teaching assistant exit through the side door carrying a large box. A briefcase dangled from one of her hands.

He sprinted down the aisle and out the back door in time to see her crossing a field outside the auditorium, heading toward a parking lot.

"Hey! Jennifer!" he shouted.

She appeared to speed up, so he ran.

"Wait, please," he said. "Let me help you." He caught up to her and wrestled the box from her hands. "I'll gladly carry this for you."

"What do you want?" she demanded. Fire flashed in her glare.

"I need to talk with Dr. Collins," he said. "Look. I wasn't totally truthful with you back there—I admit that. But I've got to talk with him. My life depends on it."

"Oh, yeah? How's that?"

"Some people are chasing me. They think I know more than I do. They've tried to kill me several times."

"Bullshit." She glared at him with skepticism. She marched on toward the parking lot. "Leave me alone. You're trouble, and I don't want to have anything to do with you."

"Just let me talk with Dr. Collins for an hour."

They had arrived at her car, and she threw the briefcase into the backseat. Clicking her key, she opened the trunk, took the box from his hands, and threw it inside. She closed the trunk and headed for the driver's side of the car.

"Please," he said. "Just let me know where to go from here. Dr. Collins is my last chance."

"Who tried to kill you?"

"I don't know. Some bald man with a black goatee. He tried to throw me into traffic first, and later, he burned down my house." It sounded far-fetched, but more realistic than "He blew up my house."

"Give me your backpack," she said but didn't wait for him to hand it over. She grabbed it from his shoulder and rifled through it, searching. After a few minutes, she discarded it to the side. She reached inside her car, fetched an object from her purse, and then turned to confront him. "Do you have a weapon?" She held a small canister of pepper spray a few inches from his face.

"Weapon? No," he said.

"Empty your pockets," she said.

He obeyed and held out some pocket change and a used bus receipt for her to see. She walked behind him and roughly patted his clothes, searching for something that he might use as a weapon.

After the search, she paused for a few seconds and studied his face again. Then she surveyed the parking lot around them. Finally, she opened the door to the backseat and said, "Turn around." She retrieved a scarf from her purse and tied it tightly over his eyes.

He heard her open the back door of the car, and she shoved him forward. "Get in."

He didn't wait for a second request as he launched into the backseat. He was desperate. She tossed his backpack in after him.

"How long have you known Dr. Collins?"

"Shut up. The less you know about me and Chris, the better."

Chris? She was on a first-name basis with the doctor. He remained quiet in the back seat.

They drove a short distance, stopping and making more turns than he sensed were really necessary. He tried to count the turns but quickly lost track. They came to a stop in a shaded area. She sat quietly, as if waiting to see if they had been followed.

"Is it clear?" Allan asked.

"Shhhh," she said. "Goddamn. Can't you shut up?"

Finally, she said, "Let's go."

He pulled off the blindfold, opened the back door, and stepped out into the late morning sunshine. They were parked in a shaded lot. Sidewalks led to different two-story apartment complexes. He looked for something that might provide more information about his location, such as a street sign or the name of the complex, but none could be seen. Jennifer was already far ahead of him, so he had to hurry to follow her into the apartment building. She fished some keys from her purse as they scaled two sets of stairs. They walked down a hallway, and she opened the apartment door and ushered him inside.

Jennifer threw her keys on the counter as she entered the kitchen. Allan walked past the kitchen to the living room. The bookshelves and furniture were basic knock-down, with a nice knick-knack here and there. It was a place any grad student would find comfortable.

"How did the lecture go, Jenn?" an older woman with short, straight gray bangs asked as she walked in from another room. She wore a T-shirt and stretch pants but no shoes. "Who the hell is this?" she asked when she saw Allan.

In an instant, Allan realized Dr. Chris Collins was a woman. He had wrongly assumed she was a man. It shouldn't have mattered, but he mentally kicked himself anyway. "I'm Allan Chappel," Allan said, offering his hand. She didn't shake it.

"Chris, he said he needed your help. He's from Atlanta," Jennifer told Dr. Collins.

"You brought him here? My God, you idiot." Her entire body tightened like a knot. She rushed to the sliding glass doors and peered out the window to see if they had been followed.

"I'm not here to hurt you," Allan said.

"You couldn't if you wanted to," Chris said. "But the people who are following you could."

"I'm pretty sure I wasn't followed. I just need some time to talk," Allan said. "Then I'll leave."

Dr. Collins eyed Allan carefully. Then, without taking her eyes off Allan, she said, "Jenn, would you mind making us some tea."

———————————

Joseph P. Strong glanced quickly around the disheveled office in disgust. Compared to his fourteenth-story corner office, Inspector Johnson's tiny, cramped quarters were a pigsty. Not one, but three towers of file folders cluttered the inspector's small desk. Photographs and memos clung to the walls with tape. Dust gathered on the base of a nearby lamp. And the smell. A putrid smell seeped out of the trash can, which was filled with leftover bags from fast food restaurants.

"Thank you, Dr. Strong, for coming in to see me today," Johnson said, slipping in behind him. He carried a single cup of steaming coffee. He didn't offer Strong anything to drink. "Please have a seat."

Strong looked for a place to sit down. One chair contained an old leather briefcase. Books and scraps of paper filled the other.

"Oh, I'm sorry," muttered Johnson. He removed the old briefcase to free up the chair for his guest. "Please have a seat here."

Strong sat uneasily in the old chair, uncertain of how dirty it might be. He looked up into the inspector's face and sensed the same feeling of disdain he had felt when he came into the inspector's office, now directed at him.

"How can I help you?" the inspector asked, almost rudely.

Strong launched into the speech he had practiced on the drive from Augusta to Atlanta. "Well, sir. I understand that you are the detective in charge of investigating the abortion clinic bombing that occurred a few days ago, here in Atlanta."

"I'm working on it. Me, and a bunch of guys around here."

"I'm sure you know about my organization, LifeWatch?"

"I've heard of it."

"We stand resolutely and unashamedly against abortion."

"I've heard that, too."

Strong sensed that it wouldn't be easy to persuade the inspector of anything the man didn't want to believe. Still, he needed to go on record. "I wanted to personally tell you that my organization does not condone the senseless violence that took place last week."

"Well, Dr. Strong," Johnson said, rubbing his hands back and forth. "No one ever said your organization had anything to do with the bombing."

"I'm aware of that. However, instead of making you come to us, I wanted to take the initiative to offer any and all of our resources to you to help you solve this case quickly and expediently."

"Thank you, sir. I'm sure your offer will be a big help to us."

"You're very welcome, Inspector," Strong said.

"I would like a list of your donors. When can I expect to receive it?"

"Uh, our donors?" The request caught Strong off guard. "We don't usually disclose our donor list. What good would—"

"It stands to reason that people who would donate their hard-earned money to fight abortion might be inclined to take deadly steps as well," the inspector said.

"I'm certain that no one affiliated with the LifeWatch organization would participate in such a despicable act."

"Let me determine that. The list?"

Strong felt backed into a corner. "I'll have my director of operations pull that together and send it to you as soon as I return home."

"Very well. And I'll need a complete contact list of your employees, including employees who have left your organization over the last three or four years. Can you send that as well?"

"I'll talk with our director of human resources," Strong said.

"I know you want to help us solve this case quickly," Johnson said, with a touch of sarcasm in his voice.

"Absolutely," Strong replied.

The inspector stood behind his desk. "Thank you for coming in, and thank you for your assistance."

He offered his hand. Strong shook it and turned for the door, feeling like a soldier who had just received his marching orders. He didn't like being dictated to. He was not used to that. He breathed in deeply, straightened his back, and left the office.

———————

"It's about Inc.Ubator," Allan said, sipping his tea. Sunlight beamed through a large sliding glass door at one end of the apartment, making the place look warmer than the reception he had received.

"Dan Carlisle's Inc.Ubator? I'm not at all surprised," Dr. Collins said. "You came up here from Atlanta to talk with me about that?"

Allan didn't like her condescending tone. It made him think she was trying to make him feel stupid. Allan was far from stupid.

"Look, you were a consultant, right?"

"Hardly," the doctor said. "I wrote an article for a professional journal. That's all."

"About stem cell research?"

"I've written dozens of articles about stem cell research," she retorted. "That's what I do, among other things."

Allan waited as patiently as a man on the run for his life could possibly wait. He knew Dr. Collins was dragging her feet.

"The piece that caught Carlisle's attention was about harvesting embryos by removing them from the uterus." Dr. Collins rubbed her long, slender fingers across her forehead, sliding her bangs to the side. "Pure speculation. We managed to successfully separate a pig embryo from the mother's womb with the placenta intact and reattach it to another gilt."

"Gilt?"

"Pregnant pig," Jennifer said from her place on the sofa.

Dr. Collins added, "Much of my work has dealt with the female reproductive system. It is important to me. Not that you, a man, would be able to understand." She tilted her chin up, and her upper lip rose just a bit.

Even though he felt as if she had just slighted him, Allan sat still. The information he wanted was more important than the pride of responding defensively to her comments. After a long pause, he said, "I imagine you are very passionate about issues relating to female reproduction. Even though I don't understand everything, I can still muster up enough empathy to understand that the subject, and any issues around it, are a priority for someone like yourself."

Dr. Collins seemed satisfied with Allan's response. She sat back in her chair. "They published my study in an issue dedicated to stem cell research. A lot of people went shit-crazy. I almost lost my grant. Only after I swore up and down that we had nothing to do with humans did the media leave us alone." She sipped from her cup.

"How did you meet Dan Carlisle?"

"After the media storm died away, I got a call from Carlisle. He gave me a lucrative contract for a very brief visit to his office in Atlanta. I told them what I knew. I explained how our process worked. I provided some details about what we had learned, and I left."

"You weren't more involved than that?"

"No."

"What went on at Inc.Ubator?" Allan asked.

"How the hell do I know? He made claims about all sorts of break-throughs. He said they'd found a way to manufacture blood."

"He told me about that."

"He also had patented some special form-fitting, sterile gloves for hospitals and doctors' offices."

"He mentioned that, too."

"Well, they're lies, all lies," Dr. Collins said angrily. "The man's lies bordered on pathological. You never should have trusted him. He'd cheat you and then blame you, every time. If his claims were true, I'd be the first to join his team, but I found him to be full of empty promises."

"What happened?"

Dr. Collins looked more than irritated. She put down her teacup, leaned forward in her chair, holding her hands as if trying to warm them over a fire, looked into Allan's face, and said, "He made impossible claims. He said they had performed miracles that medical science has tried to do without success for decades. And he promised to make us all rich. He was totally delusional. I refused to have anything else to do with him or Inc.Ubator."

"I take it you heard about the destruction of Dan's offices."

"CNN reported an abortion clinic was bombed in Atlanta," Dr. Collins said. "But I knew it was his office."

"It wasn't an abortion clinic," Allan said. "At least, that's what I thought at first. Now, I just don't know. Maybe . . ."

"That's what the newspapers called it. Anyway, I put two and two together and assumed someone put an end to his lies." Dr. Collins seemed cautious now. "By the way, what is your role in this?"

"I interviewed for a job. Communications director," he said. "Dan and I knew each other when we were in grad school."

"I see. Sorry for you." There was no empathy in her voice.

"There's more," Allan said, and the doctor seemed more agitated. She drummed her fingers back and forth on the arm of her chair.

"I believe I was targeted to be killed in the explosion at the Inc.Ubator office."

Dr. Collins tapped her foot impatiently.

"In fact, they tried to kill me twice, but I was lucky."

"Yes, I would say you were."

Allan waited again for the news to soak in. "I need some information about why people are trying to kill me."

"What did the person who tried to kill you look like?"

"The guy who jumped me was big, bald with a crunched nose, as if he'd had it broken several times. Also, he had a black goatee and a huge eagle tattoo on his chest. And he needed dental work—desperately."

"Unfortunately, that could be one of hundreds of students here at UT. Hell, half the football team is big, bald, and bearded."

"What else do you know about Inc.Ubator that might help me?"

"I really don't know much, Mr. Chappel." Her defenses seemed to be breaking down, and she appeared to accept his story. "I do know these people will be very determined. They will continue to pursue you until they find you. And when they do, they will kill you."

Her words sounded like nails in Allan's coffin.

"You should run away and hope no one ever finds you again."

"I don't have any place to run to."

"Find a place. That's why I'm here, at Jennifer's. I want to live to see tomorrow." She flashed a thin smile of appreciation Jennifer's way.

Allan started to gather his things. "Can you think of anything that might help me?"

"Let me ask you this. Who died in the office explosion in Atlanta?" Dr. Collins asked.

Allan stopped his gathering. "Well, Dr. Carlisle, Dr. Harry Ayres, three college student interns, and a receptionist."

"And no one else? Think!"

"I believe they got to Drs. Griffen and Smallwood, too." Allan held off mentioning Dr. Phillips in hopes that Dr. Collins would bring her up herself.

The professor thought for a long moment. "Yes. She may be the person you need to find," Dr. Collins said.

"Who is that?"

"On the second day of my visit with Carlisle, he had another visitor, one you haven't mentioned. I think her name was Phillips. Dr. Carole Phillips."

"There was no Carole Phillips in the Inc.Ubator office the day I visited," Allan said. "But, I found a list—"

Dr. Collins interrupted, "Carlisle made a point to introduce her as a physician as well as a researcher. As I recall, he referred to her as the organization's international liaison. He said she spoke several different languages, although I don't recall which ones. She seemed very competent."

Allan pulled out the contractor list. "I think the Dr. Phillips on this list is in Klaipeda, Lithuania. She may be able to help me find out why someone destroyed the office in Atlanta."

"They may not know about her, Allan. Obviously, they've missed some consultants. They haven't gotten me—yet."

Just then, Allan's phone began to vibrate. He read Aunt Julia's message: *Prepare for a long journey.*

"It looks like I'm going to Lithuania." He pocketed the phone. "Keep looking over your shoulder, Dr. Collins. And thank you. You've been very helpful."

Carole had faced tough times before. Her parents had died when she was in high school, but she worked hard, studied harder, and graduated from college and medical school with high honors. Her adventures in a foreign country almost came to an end when her finances ran out and she almost caved in to move back to the States, but Dan Carlisle stepped in to support her work with finances and resources, and she was able to keep her practice.

But never had she felt that her life, her very existence, was in danger—until now. Since the harrowing news from Atlanta, her nerves had been on edge like never before. Strangers made her suspicious. Slight sounds made her jump. Anything out of the norm threatened to force her back into her shell to evaluate and ponder, lest she be harmed.

The worst thing was she felt she had no options. Things were happening regardless of her response. Any choices she made would not matter. It was such a paradox—her young career was dedicated to finding new medical options, but right now she seemed to have no options herself.

She felt out of control, and this increased her risk. When people feel they have no control, they often do stupid things. Carole knew there was a difference between stupid and risky. She feared stupid. She embraced risk.

Jennifer drove Allan to the Knoxville airport. On the way, they stopped at a second-hand clothing store, and he picked up some extra clothes and an overcoat. That night, he caught a flight to New York.

Time ticked by faster than he had expected. Whenever he caught a stranger's look or heard a loud voice, he imagined the police had found him. They would, in time.

Settling into a vinyl chair at the back of the concourse, he called Aunt Julia.

"I've been waiting for your call," she said, almost as a reprimand.

"Been busy."

"Are you all right, hon?"

"I've had some close calls."

"I sense that you need to keep running. You've lost your pursuers for a while, but I don't think they will stay away for long."

"I'm going out of country."

"I know. And you're going somewhere cold," she said. "Keep warm. Be safe."

"Can you tell if I'm going to find what I'm looking for?"

"I believe you will be very satisfied, in more ways than one," she said, and her voice seemed very distant. "But there is sadness to come, too."

"I'm scared, Aunt Julia."

"I know, dear. So am I."

That night, Wesley Blake purchased a ticket to Klaipeda, Lithuania, using his Visa card. Since, like many other travelers, Allan was wearing a face mask, his disguise went undetected. The overworked airline employee hardly glanced at his passport, as did the TSA agent. He boarded the flight with little more than a backpack and a newly purchased overcoat, turning his back on Atlanta, Knoxville, the bombings, and the murders, searching for redemption in another land three thousand miles away.

SEVEN

K eith Edwards chose one of the folding chairs in the back, even though the other members of the accounting department took the seats closer to the front of the auditorium. Light rock music played in the background as the employees entered in small groups of four or five. Extra seats had been added to accommodate everyone who worked at LifeWatch.

Keith was barely seated when Joseph Strong, dressed casually in a sport jacket and golf shirt, made his way to the front of the auditorium, patting employees' shoulders in a friendly manner as he walked down the aisle. Twice, he stopped to shake the hand of a mid-level manager. Every person he touched looked up with a welcoming smile. Appearing almost reluctant to leave these people, he mounted the stage. Keith rocked back in his chair, his head resting lightly on the auditorium wall.

"Thank you all for joining me today," Strong said into the single microphone set on the stage next to a wooden stool. Uncapping a bottle of water, he took a sip and said, "I know you're all extremely busy, and I promise to make this last only as long as is absolutely necessary so you all can get back to the vital work that you do." Sincerity oozed from him.

Keith wanted to ignore the CEO of LifeWatch and allow his mind to fade into a daydream. He wanted to think about something else, anything else. He wanted to get up and walk out of the auditorium.

Strong interrupted his thoughts. "You've all heard the news about the recent bombing of an abortion clinic in Atlanta."

Murmurs rumbled through the crowd. A few employees started clapping.

Strong held up his right hand to stop the applause. "As much as we all want to celebrate the demise of one more evil, life-destroying clinic, we must take the high road. There are potential repercussions that may yet cause serious damage to our cause."

A somber silence fell among the employees.

Strong breathed deeply, which gave him a larger-than-life, authoritative stance. "Those who oppose us will try to associate this terrible act of violence with us—falsely." His gaze bounced from employee to employee. "They will try to say we caused innocent people to die. They will say we provoked this. They will try to blame us."

Keith felt uncomfortable, sitting in the back of the dimly lit auditorium. Something far in the recesses of his mind made him cautious. He couldn't put his finger on it. He couldn't identify it. He called it his bullshit alarm. For some reason, whenever Strong talked, his bullshit alarm went off.

Others around him obviously weren't wired the same way. They nodded their heads in agreement. Some muttered words of encouragement like parishioners in a church—"Yes," and "That's right."

"You need to know some things that have not yet been reported in the media," Strong said. "I want you to hear it from me, first." Keith's bullshit alarm buzzed louder.

"As I said earlier, some will try to pin this heinous deed on us. They'll point the finger at you, or at me. But you need to know that LifeWatch had absolutely nothing to do with this. We don't work that way. We are above that." An avalanche of applause rippled through the theater.

Keith found himself applauding lightly.

"Also, you need to know that the owner and head physician at the abortion clinic was a man named Daniel Carlisle." Strong paused and watched his employees. "Some of you recognize the last name. He was the son of Congressman James Carlisle, a righteous and godly man who has supported LifeWatch since its inception."

Some in the crowd looked shocked. A gasp or two could be heard in the crowded auditorium.

"Sometimes," Strong said, with lowered voice, "our children do not follow our teachings. There are members of this audience who have experienced this personally." More nods in agreement.

Somehow, the sharing of this news and the affirmative support of the other employees worked to tone down Keith's bullshit alarm. He found that he appreciated the information.

"But the most important thing is to recognize," Strong said with a firmness that only a skilled orator could muster, "recognize that we are on the right path. We would never condone such violence. We are committed to a higher calling, a higher cause. And know that we will not waver in our commitments."

Applause shook the room.

Keith joined in the applause. He wanted to be a part of the movement. He wanted to join the other employees. He stood when his peers stood. He clapped louder and harder. He agreed.

Klaipeda was a bizarre mix of old Europe, the Cold War, and the twenty-first century. Parts of the city were filled with quaint shops on narrow, cobblestone roads reminiscent of World War II. In other sections, bland Soviet-style apartment complexes made of gray, featureless concrete, often cheaply constructed and crumbling in places, were stacked on top of each other. A little farther into town, new shopping districts displayed the latest fashions from all over Europe. In fashion, black seemed to be the color *du jour*. Black coats, pants, and boots. All of the women wore boots.

Allan shrugged his own coat closer to ward off the morning cold, hoping the sun would eventually warm the day. The travel guide revealed that Klaipeda had more than fifty thousand citizens. His dilemma: how to find Dr. Carole Phillips in such a large city.

Allan checked into the Victoria Hotel Klaipėda. Although it was far more expensive than he could afford, it would do for one evening. The brand name, and its majestic stature, promised safety in a strange land. He vowed to find something more inexpensive the next day.

The hotel overlooked the Dane River and the historic section of the city beyond, called "Old Town." That night, he walked across the Mokykios Bridge and felt that he had gone back in time seventy-five years. Apartment buildings, shops, art galleries, grocery stores, and restaurants bordered cobblestone streets, lit by streetlights. Small parks containing statues of folk heroes dotted the landscape. Small boats lined the Dane River.

Allan returned to the hotel to continue his search. He sat down with the hotel concierge, an overly polite lady named Kristine. Her narrow face complemented her slender frame. Her dark hair was tugged back into a bun that further contributed to her streamlined features.

"We have two shopping malls in Klaipeda," she said proudly. "Would you like address?"

"No. I'm not here to shop. I am looking for a physician, a doctor," Allan replied. "Her name is Dr. Carole Phillips. I believe she is an American. If I could speak with someone in some hospitals, I might find someone who knows Dr. Phillips."

Kristine began writing information down on a pad of paper. "We have several hospitals in Klaipeda and many fine doctors."

He asked her to include addresses and phone numbers in the list. Within a few minutes, after searching through a directory, she handed over a complete list.

"Tomorrow, I will need someone to take me to these locations, a driver. Do you know of anyone who might do that?"

Kristine smiled. "My brother. He drives a cab. What time would you like to begin?"

"Nine-thirty," he said.

"He'll meet you in the lobby," she said. "His name is Serhiy."

EIGHT

The next morning, Allan found the sun shining more brightly than it had since his ordeal began. He took that as a positive omen. He rose, showered, dressed, and went to the restaurant at the top of the hotel for a delightful but expensive breakfast of scrambled eggs, waffles, and bacon. He looked out of the large windows at the glistening Dane River flowing below and the historic Old Town just beyond.

He returned to his room, packed his things, and went downstairs to the lobby at 9:15 to check out.

Then he received a wake up call. His phone started to vibrate, so he swiped it on. When he read Aunt Julia's text message, a feeling of impending dread flooded his soul. *Trouble. Read metro section, ajc.com.*

He tapped the link to the *Atlanta Journal-Constitution*'s website. He scrolled his way to the Metro section and read the headlines: "Search Resumes: Man Suspected of Clinic Bombing." Allan's name and photograph were displayed prominently beneath the headline. The article described how the Atlanta police were continuing the search for him concerning the bombing of the abortion clinic just a few days earlier. The article indicated that police had thought he had died in what had looked like an accidental bombing at his home, but now, the bombing seemed to have been deliberately planned to mislead the authorities.

A neighbor of his told the reporter he had had no idea an antiabortion terrorist lived next door. Allan could not recall ever meeting the man.

A colleague at the office swore that the police were looking for the wrong man. "Couldn't be him. I know Allan. He wouldn't do that. He couldn't do that."

He didn't have much time. It was pushing ten o'clock in Klaipeda, which made it about five o'clock in the morning back in Atlanta and maybe two o'clock in Arizona where Aunt Julia, awakened by one of her psychic visions, must have searched the web before grabbing her phone to send an urgent text his way.

He imagined they were interrogating Wes around the clock. The police had probably already been to Wes's house, possibly based on his emergency counseling appointment with Dr. Chamberlain. It wouldn't be long before they figured out that he had Wes's passport and credit cards as well. In time, they would trace his trip to Lithuania and would probably request that he be brought in and extradited back to the U.S. But they weren't here yet.

He returned to the lobby to wait for Serhiy. He didn't have to wait long.

"Mr. Blake?"

Serhiy didn't look to be much older than twenty. Dressed in a down-filled parka and blue jeans, he held his hand out to Allan. "My name is Serhiy. My sister said you wanted tour guide for the day."

Allan grabbed his hand. "Yes, I do."

They walked out to Serhiy's car, a late-model Toyota Corolla. "We should discuss my fees," Serhiy said, leaning over the top of the car.

Allan's flesh tingled with nervousness. They could easily trace him to the Victoria Hotel through Wes's credit cards. He needed to get off the grid, fast. He climbed in the passenger side.

"Or not," Serhiy said. He got in the car and turned the ignition. "Where to, Mr. Blake?"

"The hospital," Allan said. "Klaipeda Hospital."

"Yes, sir," his driver said, pressing the gas pedal. The tires squealed in the early morning calm.

Allan didn't look back. He didn't care to know if they were chasing him or not. He wondered what jails were like in Lithuania and whether extradition took long. If caught, he imagined being stuck here in some dingy, former Soviet hellhole for decades, subsisting on bread and water and dying of scurvy, foot-and-mouth disease, or some more exotic illness. Perhaps coming to Lithuania had been a mistake.

Serhiy parked his car in the visitor's parking lot at the first hospital. "The Klaipeda Hospital," he said and started to open his door.

Allan placed a hand on his chest and leaned in close. "Look, Serhiy. I don't think I have much time."

The young man's eyes opened wide in surprise.

"I need to find a doctor. Her name is Dr. Carole Phillips. Understand?"

He didn't blink an eyelid but nodded. "Yes. My sister mentioned this."

"I need you to come in and interpret for me."

"Yes, sir."

They walked up the sidewalk to the hospital and went inside. An armed policeman sat at a desk in the corner. He didn't look up from his magazine.

The lobby seemed to date the hospital back to the 1960s. Brown wood grain lined the walls behind vinyl chairs.

Allan approached the receptionist's desk. "Do you speak English?" The receptionist shook her head.

"Serhiy, tell her we're looking for a specific doctor."

Serhiy spoke to her in Lithuanian, "Mes ieškome daktaro vardu Karola Filips."

She shook her head.

They walked back out to the parking lot and the waiting Toyota. From there, Serhiy drove to Klaipeda University Hospital. They struck out there, and at Klaipeda Seaman's Hospital, and at the Tuberculosis Hospital. They scouted all eight hospitals in Klaipeda without finding a single person who knew of Carole Phillips.

They stopped for a late lunch at the Yellow Submarine, a large pizza restaurant in Old Town. The salads were good, but the pizza took a little getting used to. Allan had never had pizza topped with boiled eggs before.

That afternoon, Serhiy drove him to the Klaipeda post office. The building was a real tribute to early Soviet-style architecture. It resembled an old, stately government landmark on the outside, with a dark lobby just behind the front doors. Small lights mounted in candelabras overhead did little to break through the dark interior wood walls and counters.

With Serhiy's help, they inquired about a mailing address for Carole Phillips but came away disappointed. They also visited the city's two universities, Klaipeda University and LCC International University, without success.

Later that afternoon, Serhiy dropped Allan at the Litinterp Guesthouse, a quaint old bed-and-breakfast built in the 1800s. Allan chose a single room, refusing the better-priced, shared double room, and paid for two nights with cash. He knew his money reserves wouldn't last forever and resolved to find Carole Phillips as soon as possible. He had to find her before the local authorities found him.

He gave Serhiy one hundred euros, and the young man cheerfully went on his way, promising to return the next day for another search.

That night, Allan walked the streets of Old Town, taking in the sights and sounds of a magical European city. Couples walked arm-in-arm down the cobblestones, admiring shop windows and talking in soft voices. Gas streetlights seemed to light the way to a safer world.

About twenty-five years ago, Allan's father had stood beside him under the big oak tree in the backyard. Old, used lumber, retrieved from an ancient, dilapidated shack in the back corner of the yard, lay at their feet. The oak spread its mighty branches above them.

"Where should we put your treehouse?" his dad asked. To Allan, his dad looked almost as tall as the tree. At the very least, he was tall enough to jump up and touch the lowest branches.

"Way up high. As high as we can get," he said.

His dad leaned the ladder against the tree and told him, "Climb up. I'll be right behind you."

One rung at a time, Allan scaled the old wooden ladder. When he reached the top, his dad said, "Higher?"

Allan looked down toward the ground and was shocked to see how high he was. He leaned in and clung to the wood rungs for dear life.

"I don't think so," he said.

"There's a great spot about ten feet higher." His dad pointed to a place in the tree where the branches came together, then climbed up higher so that both of his arms surrounded Allan, protecting him.

"I don't think that's such a good place," Allan said. "That one's better." He pointed to a V-shaped section below them where the branch divided into two, much closer to the ground. "We could lay the boards across those branches and add a rope ladder and some walls and a roof."

"Why didn't you choose that spot when we were on the ground?" his father asked.

"I just didn't see it, Dad."

"Sometimes, it's important to see things from different perspectives, son, in order to discover all of our options. Only then do we know which is best."

They never finished the tree house. Later that summer, his mom, dad, and sister died in a multicar pileup while coming home from a dance recital. Allan was spared because he had spent the night at a friend's house.

After that, he had moved to Florida to live with his grandparents. He wanted to live with Aunt Julia in Arizona, but Grandpa wouldn't let him.

"She's a loon," he said, stifling the idea with a wave of his hand.

"She just has a different perspective," Allan argued.

"We can do without her perspectives," he said.

Maybe, for a while.

———————————

Almost all of the autumn leaves had fallen, and the roads throughout Augusta were bordered with gold, yellow, and brown stacks of colors. Strong pushed the BMW through tree-lined streets of Georgia's second oldest city.

Over the years, Strong had visited James Carlisle's home on several social and political occasions. His house could be the backdrop in *Gone with the Wind*, with large faux columns and stately grounds, surrounded by a spotlessly white clapboard fence to keep the farm animals in and other animals out.

A housekeeper, young and attractive, opened the door when Strong knocked. "The Carlisles are not taking any visitors today," she announced.

Strong quickly interrupted her. "I'm here to share my condolences with James. My name is Joseph Strong." His confident tone seemed to be the key.

She appeared a bit unsure of how to proceed and said, "Please wait a moment. I will be right back."

Almost immediately the door opened again, and James Carlisle's massive figure filled the frame. "Joseph Strong. So good of you to come." He extended his hand to shake Strong's hand and followed his handshake with a less-than-comfortable hug.

"In times like this it's important for friends to support each other." Strong tried to focus on Carlisle's eyes, to show sympathy.

The congressman's face lit up. "Yes, you are so right," he said in an unquestionably Southern drawl. "Please come in."

The two men walked arm-in-arm through the foyer to an attractively formal family room where they sat on sofas and chairs that had seldom known the warmth of a man or woman's buttocks. One of the staff brought pastries and iced tea, and Strong felt as welcome as a Southern boy who had come home for good.

Congressman Carlisle looked to Strong with a deeply concerned expression on his face and said, "Joseph, I'm glad you came by."

"I was very sorry to hear about Daniel's death," Strong said. "What a tragic loss of life for someone who had so much to live for."

Carlisle nodded and refocused the conversation. "Helen is so upset. It'll take a long time for her to recover." He stared at the floor.

Strong had practiced his lines over and over on the drive. He paused for a respectful moment and said, "It must be doubly painful, knowing your son operated such a heinous practice."

"I beg your pardon?"

"Abortions. You must be very sad about Dan performing abortions."

"Joseph," Carlisle said. "Dan did not perform abortions."

"All of the news outlets say he did."

"In fact," Carlisle added, "he tried to prevent abortions."

Strong took a calculatedly deep breath and proceeded cautiously. "James, whatever he did cannot be undone. Your sacred name has been tarnished by the media beyond repair. Public opinion has logged the vote and has decided the sins of the son are also the sins of his father. In a situation like this, you can never go back. The damage has been done."

Congressman Carlisle remained stoically silent.

"I know you to be a righteous man," Strong continued. "And your supporters will remember you in the same manner."

"But Dan's work—"

"What happened to your son is tragic. Whoever did this should be treated as harshly as the law will allow," Strong said. "But it won't bring him back. There is just no way to turn back the hands of time."

The congressman began to cry. His ruddy cheeks shuddered as tears rolled down his face.

"I believe you and your lovely wife Helen need time to mourn, and to heal." Strong paused again. The congressman continued to weep, uncontrollably. Strong reluctantly rested a firm palm on his shoulder.

"But it is possible to move ahead," Strong continued. "You need someone who will follow in your impressive congressional footsteps and deflect the public opinion away from you and your grieving wife, Helen. Someone who will champion your tireless cause for the unborn but will not allow the progressive media to slander the name of James Carlisle further."

A knowing look crossed Carlisle's face.

"James," Strong continued, afraid to give up a moment lest doubt creep into the congressman's thoughts, "you and I share the same traditional values. We share the same passion and the same love for our country. Let me help you and your family heal. Let me help our wonderful district heal by championing your cause and protecting your name."

The congressman stared at the floor for a long, long time. Strong feared he may have overstepped his bounds. But, when the deafening silence became almost unbearable, James Carlisle spoke.

"Yes. You are right."

Joseph P. Strong's journey continued. A crooked smile crept over his lips as he headed forward, reaching for his destiny.

Allan was stumped, frightened, three thousand miles away from home, and wanted for multiple murders. Somewhere, a big, bald man wanted to kill him. Allan sat in a neat little bed-and-breakfast in a foreign country, having an early morning breakfast of bagels, eggs, and ham, waiting for that knock on the door, the tap on the shoulder, or the innocuously kind word that would begin his arrest proceedings.

Serhiy had said he would pick him up at around nine. They were going to try to visit some government organizations and locate Dr. Phillips.

The day was bright and crisp, though a chilly minus-nine degrees Celsius. Bundled in a jacket and overcoat, Allan walked out the front door to do a little pre-search exploring. He walked up the street from his hotel and watched the people coming and going. Few citizens in Klaipeda seemed to use or own cars. Most took public transportation—specifically, city buses. He was amazed at how many children, some apparently as young as six or seven, rode the bus unaccompanied.

Serhiy had said children could ride for free. They traveled to school by city bus every morning. Still, it surprised Allan to see a young child walk through the back streets and alleys and hop aboard the nearest city bus without an adult nearby.

Several blocks away from the bed-and-breakfast, Allan turned the corner and ran into a mass of kids of all ages, walking together toward a nearby bus stop. Bundled in thick parkas, scarves, and boots and carrying book bags and lunch boxes, they were so totally oblivious of him that they almost ran him over.

He looked up the street in the direction from which they came and saw another mob of kids turn onto the sidewalk and head in his direction. It seemed odd that so many children would be walking to the bus together in this part of the city. He walked up the street to the point where the kids had entered the sidewalk and saw a large house surrounded by a short brick fence. A plaque on the fence announced something in Lithuanian, but he couldn't translate the name, given his limited knowledge of the language. Inside the fence, a playground flanked one wall and a stand of trees the other. As he watched, a third group of children burst through the front door and headed his way. They passed him without acknowledging his presence and trotted up the street to the bus stop.

Allan returned to Litinterp Guesthouse and sat down to a cup of hot tea while he waited for Serhiy.

Within fifteen minutes, Serhiy walked through the front door with a large smile on his face. "Are you ready to go, Mr. Blake?" he asked, with as much enthusiasm as anyone could possibly muster. The guy had a great attitude. "I have collected ten doctors' addresses that we could visit on this day."

"Great, Serhiy. But I have a detour first."

"Yes, sir." No more questions.

They got in his Toyota, and Allan directed him up the street where he had walked earlier. They pulled to the side of the road in front of the house with the low brick fence. "Serhiy, what is this place?"

Serhiy looked through the driver's window at the plaque on the wall.

"That is private orphanage."

"Really?"

"Yes. We have several in Klaipeda. Some have their own schools. In others, children attend public schools."

Allan mulled over that for a moment. Orphanages would often be in need of a doctor. Perhaps someone would know of Dr. Carole Phillips.

"Serhiy, I want to visit orphanages."

"Sir?" He gave Allan the oddest look.

"Yes. We'll start here. Orphanages need doctors, for birthing infants and caring for sick kids. Let's go inside."

They walked up to the front porch and knocked on the wooden door.

A large, paunchy woman came to the door, wearing a sweatsuit beneath a red apron. Flour covered the front of the apron.

"Labas?" she said.

"Labas rytas," Serhiy said. "Ar galėčiau paklausti jūsų vieno ar dviejų klausimų?"

She said, "Ya."

"Mes ieškome daktaro vardu Karola Filips."

The large lady shook her head, "No."

Serhiy looked at Allan a moment and then said, "Mano draugas su ja mokėsi viename universitete."

She began to nod. "Yes." A faint smile crossed her lips, and she winked at Allan. Then she began to speak again.

Serhiy took out a pen and notepad and began to jot down notes.

They both shook hands with the lady and turned to walk back to the car. "What was that all about?"

"I asked her if she knew the doctor named Carole Phillips. She did not but wanted to know why we were asking. So I told her you were an American doctor and you met her at conference in Sweden. You lost her address but wanted to see her again, so we were asking around."

Allan thought about it a moment. The explanation was as good as any he could have come up with. He nodded. "Good job, Serhiy."

"Oh, and she gave me names and addresses of five other orphanages in Klaipeda which we may want to inquire."

"Very good job. What are we waiting for?"

———————————

They spent most of the day knocking on doors, asking if people knew Carole Phillips, and moving on. Or at least Serhiy did. Allan just stood by and watched. Serhiy continued to use the doctor-looking-for-a-doctor ruse, and it worked. They received the names and addresses of two infant homes and four special schools for orphans.

Finally, late in the day, they were both beginning to think they were heading down the wrong path. Serhiy crossed another name off their list as they approached a small house with a yard full of children's toys. Serhiy rang the doorbell.

A middle-aged lady came to the door. She looked tired. Her eyes were bloodshot, and there were wrinkles around them.

Serhiy introduced himself in Lithuanian. He asked if she spoke English.

"Yes," she said. "I speak English." She turned to Allan.

"We are looking for a doctor named Carole Phillips. Would you know her?" Allan asked.

"What if I did? Why do you want to see her?"

Allan froze. His heart pounded in his chest. The day's fatigue, brought on by hours of ineffective searching, faded away like the morning fog. This was the lead they were hoping for. "I'm an American."

"Yes."

"Carole and I went to school together. I'm vacationing in Europe and wanted to look her up."

She sized him up and down and up and down again. "I don't believe you." She began to close the door.

"No. Wait," Allan said. Desperately, he changed his approach. "I need to talk with her. My life may depend upon it."

A crooked smile crossed her face. "That sounds a little, er, dramatic."

"You have no idea," he said. "I really need to talk with her." He took Serhiy's pen and pad and wrote down his name and cell phone number. He also wrote the word "Inc.Ubator" and "Dan Carlisle."

"As soon as you can, contact her and ask her to call me at this number. Tell her it is about Inc.Ubator and Dan Carlisle," he said, pointing to Dan's name.

"I will give it some thought," she said and closed the door.

Allan looked at Serhiy. "I can't believe it. This means she really is here in Klaipeda."

"Wait. You did not know if she was in Klaipeda?"

Allan started laughing. "Not till now."

Serhiy took him back to Litinterp Guesthouse and gave him his cell number. "If you want to continue tour, call me."

Allan paid him another hundred euros and said goodnight.

That night, Allan dined in a delightful restaurant called Memelis. He kept the cell phone beside him the entire time. It did not ring, but he was still hopeful. Dr. Carole Phillips must be nearby.

————————————

Of all the offices at LifeWatch, none were more nicely arrayed than Joseph Strong's. Keith had only ventured into this office once before. Now, he took in the blatant opulence of Strong's furniture, awards, and trappings while standing in the doorway, politely waiting while Strong completed a phone call.

"I understand that you wanted to talk with me," Joseph Strong said as Keith entered his office.

The confrontation caught Keith off guard. He had intended to be on the attack, challenging the powerful man in his own luxurious office.

Instead, he found himself feeling defensive. "Uh, yes, sir. I do."
"Please have a seat," Strong commanded.

Keith sat in one of several plush office chairs facing the massive and spotlessly empty desk.

"What's on your mind?"

"Well," Keith began. He shuffled through some notes in file folders on his lap and cursed himself for not being more organized. "I, uh, noticed a discrepancy with several of our accounts."

"Yes?"

"There seem to be some substantial funds placed in special accounts that don't appear on our master books."

"How much are we talking about?"

"Several hundred thousand dollars."

Strong expressed little interest. "Have you talked with your supervisor?"

"No, sir. I felt that I should bring this directly to you." He placed one of the sheets on Strong's desk. "These accounts have been accessed by a former employee in our security department named Sheffield."

"I see," Strong replied. He glanced at the sheet and then set it aside. "I'll take care of this. Thank you for bringing it to my attention."

Keith did not appreciate being dismissed without being heard. "It's a lot of money."

"Yes, it is. We'll find out what is going on." Keith hesitated. "Is there anything else?"

"Well, uh, no, sir." He stood to leave. "It's just that, with the recent events in Atlanta, I'm concerned that we might face tighter federal scrutiny, and that such discrepancies might seem suspicious." He played the protection card, hoping it would gain traction.

"You certainly don't think we had anything to do with the abortion clinic bombing, do you?"

Keith's bullshit alarm sounded again. "No, sir, I'm sure LifeWatch had nothing to do with that. It just seems that we might be targeted for some sort of investigation, given the nature of that tragedy." It seemed to work.

Strong stared into Keith's eyes. "Well, rest assured that we had absolutely nothing to do with that horrific incident. We do not condone violence, regardless of how vile and despicable the abortionists' behaviors. Is that clear?" His response sounded rehearsed.

"Yes, sir."

"Thank you again for bringing this to my attention." Strong stood up, paper in hand. Keith's time was up.

"You're welcome, sir." Keith stood and walked back through the office door. Once outside, he shifted his file folder from one hand to the next. Sweat covered the bottom of the folder where his hand had been.

A lilting chime woke Allan. His phone showed that it was 1:30 in the morning. A call was coming in. "Hello?"

"Who are you?" a female voice said.

He became instantly and completely awake. "My name is Allan Chappel. Dan Carlisle was my friend. He offered me a job with Inc.Ubator. I was with him the day he died."

"How do I know you are telling the truth?"

"Look it up online. The Atlanta Journal-Constitution called the office an abortion clinic."

"I've already read the articles." Another long pause. "What do you want from me?"

Allan fought to find the best words. "Whoever killed Dan and the others is trying to kill me. They may be after you. I need to talk with you to find out who is behind this."

"I have no way of knowing that. How do I know you're not behind this?"

Allan didn't have an answer. "Perhaps if we work together, we can figure it out."

"Meet me at Jogunde at nine o'clock tomorrow morning. Come alone."

"How will I recognize you?"

"I know what you look like."

"But how—"

The phone clicked in his ear.

NINE

Jogunde was a cross between a Denny's and a nice restaurant. Light wood tabletops and clean tile floors welcomed people as they came to and from the offices and shops along the main street. Allan hustled in, away from the cold Baltic winds, and looked about the place, not sure what to look for. No one smiled a welcoming smile. No one raised her hand to wave him over to her table.

He moved toward the back of the restaurant and took a seat at a small booth in the corner.

Businesspeople came and went. An attractive woman walked by his booth and smiled at him. When he started to speak, she moved on to another table. He ordered coffee and decided to wait it out. At almost ten o'clock, someone placed a piece of paper in front of him. It was a print from the Atlanta Journal-Constitution online article about the explosion at Inc.Ubator. A drawing that bore a dead-on resemblance to Allan took up two columns. He felt the sweat break out on his forehead. Time was not on his side.

He looked up to see an attractive blonde wearing dark sunglasses and a heavy black overcoat.

He smiled at her, but she didn't smile back. She studied him closely, as he assumed she had done for the last hour.

"Dr. Phillips?" Allan stood and offered his hand.

Slowly, she extended hers and gently grasped his. She had slender, soft hands—the hands of a doctor. "Are you Allan?"

"Yes. I'm Allan Chappel," he said. "I am so glad to meet you. I've come a long way."

"Yes, you have. I hope you aren't disappointed."

There was no chance of that. Like most of the women of Klaipeda, Carole was very attractive. However, her accent betrayed her as being American, not Lithuanian. "Would you like a cup of coffee?" he asked.

"Yes." She took off her overcoat, revealing a beige sweater. She sat opposite him. A stunning necklace of gleaming brown, irregularly shaped stones strung together along a fine gold chain circled her neck.

He signaled to the waitress and ordered another cup.

Carole took off her glasses, and he welcomed the change. Her eyes were a vivid shade of green. "What was your connection to Daniel Carlisle?" she asked.

"I knew Dan when we were both in graduate school at Emory in Atlanta. We were close friends with a girl who took her life while we were in school. About a week ago, Dan invited me to interview for a position as communications director for Inc.Ubator in Atlanta."

"What were you doing before that?"

"I am, or was, in public relations for another company."

"Did you accept Dan's position?"

"I never had the chance. I met with him and later with the psychiatrist, Dr. Chamberlain. Before I could return to his office, someone destroyed the building, and I've been running since then."

"It sounds like you were very lucky."

"More than you can imagine," he said. "Later that evening, someone tried to kill me. He pushed me into traffic. That night, he drugged me in my home and planted explosives. I barely got out alive."

"Sounds a bit hard to believe," she said, and he wasn't sure if she affirmed or mocked him. "What do you know of Daniel's work?"

"Very little." He took a sip of coffee. "But what I've heard is quite impressive. I hoped I could learn more in order to find out why I'm being chased. You consulted with him, right?"

She ignored the question. "How did you find me?"

He pulled his phone from his pocket and showed her the pictures of the documents from Dr. Chamberlain's file. "I got these from Dr. Chamberlain." He didn't say they were stolen. "Dan had mentioned your name briefly in our meeting." He showed her the list of consultants. "Almost everyone on that list died this week," he said, watching her reaction. "Except you and Dr. Collins."

She sat emotionless, studying the pages, one by one. "You searched me out with nothing more than this to go on?"

"I am desperate. As I said, someone is trying to kill me. And, as you know, I'm being set up as the one who murdered these people."

She looked him dead in the eyes. "How do I know you didn't?"

"You don't," he said. "But do you think I would share all this background information with you if I had?"

"People do stupid things these days."

"Yes, they do."

Just when he feared Carole would get up and walk away, she said, "I've worked for Dan and his organization from time to time."

"Can you tell me what you did for Dan?"

"I'm a physician. I offered advice on some of his projects."

"Just hear me for a moment. Help me figure this thing out. Then, if you don't trust me, we'll go our separate ways."

"Fair enough," she said.

"Do you know if Dan had any enemies?"

"Don't we all?" she asked.

"But can you think of anyone who would hate him enough to kill him?"

She shook her head. "Can you?"

"No," he said. "If I could just find out who is behind this, I might be able to expose them and get off the hook myself. For the life of me, I just can't think of anyone who would want to kill Dan or destroy his research."

"Perhaps he has a competitor, someone who is trying to perfect similar processes," Carole said. "After all, it may be worth millions to anyone who developed it."

"But why would they be after me? I don't know anything about his organization."

"They don't know that, Allan. They must think you know more than you do." He saw concern and sympathy in her eyes and knew she was right. He had considered the same thing himself.

Her eyes darted about the room, as if trying to discern whether someone had noticed them. "Let's go for a walk," she said.

He paid for the coffee. They put on overcoats, caps, scarves, and gloves and stepped out into the windy Klaipeda air. Flurries of snow floated about in the morning breeze.

They strolled beside large plate glass windows showing European fashions on slender mannequins. One store sold nothing but ladies' boots. Another offered glasses and contact lenses. A third housed a copy center.

She talked about her college education at the University of Michigan. He talked about Emory. She was surprised to hear that he had once been a theology student.

They passed a couple of Soviet-era parks containing monolithic statues reminiscent of the Soviet Union. A third park displayed a statue of a Lithuanian fisherman. Carole explained that Klaipeda, Lithuania's only seaport, was home to thousands of fishermen.

"Tell me how you came to live in Lithuania, Carole," he said.

She walked a bit farther, as if trying to decide how much of herself to reveal. "When I was in high school back in Chicago, I learned about the fall of the Soviet Union. The story of Lithuania, and how it seceded from the Soviet Union and became an independent nation, fascinated me, as did stories of other former-Soviet Union states—Poland, Ukraine . . ." Her voice cracked. "The older generation, those who had been oppressed by the Nazis during World War II, and later by the Soviets, had given up hope."

"Certainly after that, things changed, right?"

"Not for the older generation." She turned to face him. "But the young people, those who were my age and younger, they held onto hope and dreams. They loved democracy and capitalism. They are literally the future of Lithuania. I came here to set up my practice to help them."

To Allan, her answer revealed more than a history lesson. It showed her heart.

As they walked through the older part of the city, she began to tell him tales of people she knew here and there. "Giedrius works as a shoe repairman in that shop," she said, pointing. "He's repaired shoes all his life. He made these as good as new," she said, lifting one slender foot to reveal a new sole.

"Irina recently graduated from Klaipeda University with a degree in business," she said, nodding toward a gift shop near the river. "Jobs are so scarce; even with a degree, the best she can find is part-time work here. Last year, she had her first child, a boy. I delivered him," she said with pride.

"Do you deliver many children?"

"From time to time," she said. "Irina's husband, a big, burly man named Julios, works as a chef in Forto Dvaras, across the street. He used to be a fisherman, but when she became pregnant, she put a stop to that. When he's with his son, that giant becomes as playful as a puppy."

Allan found himself fascinated with this attractive woman whose heart beat for a people now filled with hope. He enjoyed watching her eyes light up as she shared stories of life in this foreign town. He envied her. She had made a life for herself here, thousands of miles away from her Chicago home.

He also feared for her. If they came after him, they would probably come after her, too.

———————————

Keith carelessly shook three more tablets into his palm and slung them back, followed by a chug of Coke from a plastic cup. Looking over his shoulder gave him a migraine.

He left the semi-messy restaurant lobby on Watkins Street and headed back to the LifeWatch offices on Broad Street. It was a short walk, and he and many other employees of the organization often took advantage of the mild fall afternoons to slip out of the building and grab a quick, and sometimes not-so-quick, lunch. The bright sunlight made his eyes hurt more, countering any effect of the Tylenol he had just devoured.

"Hey!"

Keith turned quickly in the direction of the shout and backed instinctively away. He recognized no one. A road construction worker had called to some friends.

Still, he couldn't shake the feeling that someone was watching him. He surveyed the face of the LifeWatch wristwatch on his arm and noticed that he still had twenty minutes before his lunch hour ended and he would be expected to be back at his cubicle, crunching numbers and adding totals from donors around the world. He chose to make use of the extra time and continued walking west on Watkins. He'd take advantage of the time to find out if someone was following him.

He marched on with purpose, past closed shops and bustling parking lots. At Second Street, he turned right and continued walking away from his office building. On his left, Cedar Grove Cemetery stood, with its ivory white headstones shaded here and there by well-groomed trees and bushes. On his right was Magnolia Cemetery, with more headstones and even more trees and bushes. He had learned in elementary school that Cedar Grove was originally constructed for the black citizens of Augusta and Magnolia Cemetery was exclusively for white citizens. Both contained graves from the early 1800s.

Keith walked quickly down Second Street, trying hard to focus his attention away from the gravestones on either side of him and to any noises that might be made by someone walking immediately behind him. Halfway down the street he stopped suddenly and turned around. No one was there. He stood completely still for five minutes, watching to see if a pursuer might dart out from behind a bush or tree or street entrance, but no one showed. A chain-link fence bordered the cemetery on his left and a four-foot-high brick wall surrounded the one on his right. He walked ahead just a bit and turned left into Cedar Grove Cemetery through an open gate. He marched straight across the cemetery, surrounded by graves too numerous to count.

Again, halfway through the cemetery, he stopped abruptly and turned around. No one was there.

Frustrated, tired, and a bit clammy due to his forced early afternoon march, he turned around and retraced his steps, turning right on Second Street and heading back toward the LifeWatch offices. All throughout his trek, the feeling that someone was following him nagged him incessantly.

Eventually, Carole said she needed to get back to her work. "There are some items I need to attend to. They can't wait," she said.

"Would you let me take you to dinner this evening? We have so much more to talk about. This, today, has been so helpful to me."

"I don't know," she said with a raised eyebrow. "After all, you are a fugitive from justice."

"I promise to behave."

"Okay. Seven o'clock at Zuvine. It's a delightful seafood restaurant. Klaipeda has the best fish in the world."

Allan said goodbye and headed back to the Litinterp Guesthouse. On the way, he called Serhiy to tell him the good news. "I found her, Serhiy! The lady at the last orphanage we visited knew Carole Phillips and had her contact me."

"This is great," Serhiy said. "I assume you will not be needing another tour, then?"

"You never know. I'll keep your number handy, just in case."

He walked on back to the guesthouse. Just as he arrived, his phone chimed. He swiped it on and read the text message from Aunt Julia: *I sense happiness and friendship and . . . possibly affection?*

He sent a text back to her: *Having a wonderful time.*

Aunt Julia never bothered asking where he was. He knew she was aware that he was out of the country, but his specific whereabouts were not her concern. They both knew she could reach him, one way or another, if she needed to.

He sipped a cup of tea in the study by a window that looked out over a tiny park nestled between several apartment buildings. The park had two strange, life-sized granite statues of cats. One was walking along the top of a wall. The other was lying beneath a bench. It was as if someone had captured a perfect moment, and the cats were forever preserved for all to see.

He longed for such permanence. If he could just capture this perfect moment, and never have to face the trials that were stalking him, all would be well.

But that was not about to happen.

TEN

It made absolutely no sense. Her life, suddenly thrown into upheaval by events thousands of miles away, seemed to be severely limited in options. It unnerved her, as it would anyone.

However, and fortunately for her, she had current obligations that kept her busy—kept her from giving up and running away, which she longed to do.

And now she was faced with a new distraction. Allan Chappel first appeared in her life as life-threatening. But in the brief time she had known him, she found him intriguing. His story, as implausible as it first seemed, now resonated with her.

Someone was obviously destroying her former employer by systematically killing consultants and staff, one by one. Logic would suggest she was next, but something about Allan, something disarming and trustworthy, made his story seem true.

Even if it weren't true, her future was tenuous at best. But the cause, one she had embraced from Dan Carlisle, was a vital one and worth the potential danger. She vowed to proceed. But with caution.

Allan arrived outside Zuvine at 5:30. It seemed that his journey to Lithuania somehow shielded him, if only for a time, from the dangers back home in Atlanta. He walked past the restaurant and played tourist, taking in the sights, sounds, and smells of this seaport city. A brochure he had found in a park said that Klaipeda was not directly on the Baltic Sea but was separated from the Baltic by a large island called the Curonian Spit. Ship traffic filled the waterway between the mainland and the island. He spent an hour watching the massive boats come and go, always looking over his shoulder for anything suspicious.

Zuvine seemed to amplify his waterfront experience. The smell of fish cooked in all types of sauces and oils was incredible.

Allan was early, so he switched on his phone and caught a news video from CNN. Congressman James Carlisle spoke to reporters in a large and crowded hallway.

"As all of you know, the recent events have been difficult for Helen and me," he explained. "We both feel like our time to step aside has come. We've fought the good fight, and we're proud of the work we have accomplished for the great state of Georgia and for our wonderful country." He closed his brief press conference by mentioning that he would make an announcement soon to endorse another candidate to replace him.

Allan leaned against the restaurant wall and contemplated this bit of news. He wondered if the news about Dan's work had shamed his father into stepping down. More importantly to Allan, he wondered if the congressman knew who had destroyed Dan's offices, and if he would help Allan if asked.

Carole arrived a little before seven, dressed in a beige top with a revealing neckline, dark brown slacks, her black overcoat, and boots. She also wore the same shimmering brown stone necklace.

They were seated near a glowing fireplace. He took the chair closest to the open hearth so that he could scan the other customers. He ordered wine. For a brief moment, they let their guard down, but just a little.

"I just love this city," she said, looking out the windows onto the Dane River.

"It's fascinating," he said. "There's a little garden outside my guesthouse that has two stone statues of cats."

"Oh, I've seen that. I can't imagine why it's there. But I love cats," she said wistfully. "I always had cats when I grew up near Chicago."

"We only had one cat when I was growing up, and he didn't last very long," he added. "I've thought about getting a dog, recently. Maybe a rescue."

"My brother has a black lab. He lives on a large farm in Indiana."

"Do you have any other brothers or sisters?"

"No. He's my only living relative."

"I can relate," he said. "My Aunt Julia in Arizona is my only living relative."

"It's kind of lonely, isn't it?"

He nodded. Small talk about personal histories opened doors to more important subjects, and Allan discovered he felt a unique attraction to this international transplant from Chicago. He wondered if his interests were real or just born from the loneliness, stresses of his current situation, and his isolation from all that was familiar and welcome back home.

They had more wine, and then the waiter brought the main course. The sea bass, swordfish, potato cakes, and fresh vegetables were superb.

As the conversation began to settle, and those around them moved on to other places, he said, "Tell me about your necklace. Those are fascinating shiny stones."

"You like this?" She ran her fingers over it. "Don't know if you can call them stones. They are one of Klaipeda's most famous natural resources. Someone called them Lithuania's only natural gem."

He leaned forward and looked more closely at the coffee-colored jewelry. "They look like stones to me." He reached out, lightly lifted one between his finger and thumb, and rubbed it gently. "Feels like a stone." Yet it seemed slightly transparent, almost like quartz.

Carole laughed. "It's amber, Allan."

"Amber?"

"Yes, amber," she said. "Pine trees along the Baltic Sea give off an unusually large amount of sap, which falls into the waters and fossilizes. Lithuanians have collected amber that has washed up on the shore for centuries. Some say the amber has unusual healing powers. I've seen teething and healing necklaces used by mothers and their children. It's a fascinating product."

"It's absolutely gorgeous," he said, admiring both the necklace and the woman wearing it.

"This is one of my favorite pieces," she said. "One day, I'd like to pass it along to a daughter." A sadness seemed to appear in her eyes. "Hopefully, one day."

They wandered through the brightly lit Old Town until the night air became too cold to stand. They shared hot chocolate at Sokoladine, a delightful sweets shop, and he kissed her under stately old streetlights in one of the most enchanting cities in the world.

He told her goodnight on the bridge over the Dane River and returned to the guesthouse for the night.

He switched on his phone and dialed Aunt Julia's number. He didn't like to spend the money for overseas calls, but some occasions were worth celebrating with special relatives.

Aunt Julia didn't pick up the phone. He checked his watch. It was just after eleven o'clock, so it should have been late afternoon in Arizona. He found it odd that she didn't answer the phone because she always kept her cell phone nearby.

"Aunt Julia. Hi, this is Allan. Just wanted you to know that I am making progress, and I've met a wonderful woman. But you already know that. Call me when you can."

Allan hung up the phone and felt more alone than he had in twenty years.

Keith stared into his almost-empty whiskey glass and muttered out loud, "Where would you spend four or five hundred thousand dollars?"

"The wife would spend it before I had a chance," the bartender announced, filling Keith's glass with more of the copper liquid.

"But what if you were a business?" Keith heard his words slur and realized he was reaching his limit.

The bartender paused. "I don't know. That kind of cash can make a big dent. What's changed?"

Keith slurped the whiskey. "Nothing, really. Just some building blew up."

"I could blow up a building for less than two hundred grand," the bartender said.

Keith pondered that a moment. "But why would you do it?" he asked.

"Guess I hated the building."

"Or something inside it," Keith whispered.

"I just called a cab for you, bud," the bartender said. "Ready to settle up?"

Keith handed over the payment, slid off the stool, and headed for the door.

"Hope you find your money," the bartender called.

"I kinda hope I don't," Keith muttered.

ELEVEN

Allan awoke in the Litinterp Guesthouse the next morning. A brilliant sun shone full on a light powder covering the courtyard outside his window. He climbed out of bed, washed in the tiny shower, and went downstairs for breakfast.

He read the US newspapers on his phone. No one knew the whereabouts of the man who had bombed the abortion clinic in Atlanta. The Falcons had lost again. Trouble continued to fester in the Middle East.

Examining the guests in the small dining room, he realized he knew nothing about them. In the States, things had become so toxic, he would have wondered if the people around him were Republican or Democrat, or if they opposed vaccines or supported gun laws. Here, everyone was anonymous . . . and safe.

He resolved to get some answers from Carole today. They were meeting for lunch, and he planned to be firm and persistent. He wanted to know about her involvement with Dan Carlisle's organization and whether she could help him determine who had tried to kill him. And he was growing more attracted to her. At first, he had chalked that up to his own loneliness, but as time went on, he realized he wanted to know as much about her as he could.

Carole greeted him with a half-hug in the lobby of the guesthouse. "Come with me," she said. "I have so much to show you."

They walked down aging brick streets through Old Town until they came upon an open courtyard. One of the buildings nearby displayed an expansive balcony that overlooked the courtyard. A fountain occupied the center of the courtyard. A pillar in the fountain held a statue of a young girl, probably in her early teens, maybe younger.

"This is Anike," Carole said. "Legend has it that the German poet, Simon Dach, took one look at her and fell in love. One of his most famous poems, 'Anke von Tharaw Oss, de my fallout,' was said to have been about her. Anike has been a symbol of hope and beauty for the people of Klaipeda for a century. They erected this fountain and statue in her honor."

"Wow. She looks so young."

"But you don't know the whole story," Carole added. "During World War II, Adolf Hitler visited Klaipeda. They say he spoke to the crowds here in Theater Square from that balcony." She pointed toward the large terrace behind the statue.

Allan looked at the building across the terrace and could almost imagine Der Fuhrer shouting at the citizens of Klaipeda from behind the rail.

"Some say he was so offended that the statue of Anike had her back to the balcony where he was to speak, he had it taken down. Others say the Germans simply tore it down during the war. At any rate, it disappeared in the mid-1940s. When Lithuania seceded from the Soviet Union in 1991, the citizens raised money to have the statue restored."

They shared a late lunch in The Black Cat restaurant, sitting together at a little table upstairs and talking about the sights and the city. Then, Allan turned the conversation to more serious matters.

"Carole. You know, you grilled me pretty seriously the other day, and you dodged my questions pretty effectively."

She paused. Her cheeks reddened slightly, and she said, "I'm sorry if I was harsh, but you must understand that I need to be cautious. But I believe I can trust you now. What would you like to know?"

"For starters, you seem to be an unknown in the medical community here. I checked with every hospital and clinic in Klaipeda. No one knew a Dr. Carole Phillips. Why couldn't I find anyone here who knew you?"

"A few years after I arrived here and established my private practice, the funds ran out. This young democratic country and its low-wage earners couldn't afford my services. I thought I'd have to return to the States and start over. I was heartbroken."

She paused a moment longer. "Then Dan Carlisle offered to support my work here. We met and formed an alliance."

"I knew it. So, you did work for Dan."

"I couldn't help it. I loved Klaipeda and didn't want to return to the United States. Dan offered me a chance to stay here in return for some consulting time. Besides, he is, or was, a very persuasive guy."

"What did you do, as a consultant?"

Carole scratched the top of the wooden table in a rhythmic motion, as if trying to claw up the words to express herself. Finally, she looked up with a knowing glow on her face. "Come with me."

She took his arm and steered him deeper into Old Town. As they walked over cobblestone streets, she picked up the pace. They turned down one alleyway, and she stopped in front of a narrow apartment building that seemed to belong in an old World War II movie. With a set of keys from her overcoat, she unlocked the huge wooden door and, with a shove, it creaked open.

Complete darkness filled the entryway. Carole fumbled for another key. Allan heard it slide into the lock. She opened the second door and reached in to switch on the light.

"Welcome to Inc.Ubator II," she said.

Dan's office in Atlanta had been luxuriously furnished, and Dr. Chamberlain's office had been spartan. But the facilities of Inc.Ubator II were bleak at best. The furniture was obviously second- or third hand. Bookshelves and tables had been crudely made from pine planks. Old lamps were the primary source of light in the somewhat dim room.

"I have an apartment on the next floor up," Carole said.

Allan stumbled into the office almost in a trance. Large cabinets lined the back wall of the expansive room.

Carole turned to face Allan.

"Allan, we read the American papers here in Lithuania and throughout Europe. Most of my friends are shocked and concerned by the polarized nature of your—of our country."

"Yeah," Allan said. "There are some pretty heated opinions in the States. But what does that have to do—"

"For example," Carole interrupted, "the pro-life versus pro-choice debate. Everyone believes so passionately in their own side that they never seek an alternative, right?"

"What? How can there be an alternative? Either you're pro-life or pro-choice."

She shook her head gently. "Dan found another way. This is where he built the Inc.Ubator prototype," she said. "The laws and procedures in the States were too restrictive to try the procedure on human embryos there. Here in Lithuania, where three thousand children are placed in institutional care each year, and six thousand children grow up in institutions, the laws are much less restrictive. The government has such a hard time managing its current case load that we managed to work without government restrictions."

"I still don't understand," he said.

She couldn't contain herself. "Come with me." She turned and opened a side door.

This room bore little resemblance to a real laboratory. Several laptop computers were churning away along one wall. Some electronic monitoring equipment sat on a shelf in the back. Blue light bulbs cast an eerie glow around a table in the middle of the room.

A velvet drape covered a large object in the center of the table.

"What the hell?"

Carole smiled. "Would you like to meet one of the next citizens of Klaipeda?" she asked.

Without waiting for his answer, she slowly pulled the drape back. Beneath it sat a glass orb filled with some sort of liquid. In the dim light, he could see an object in the liquid.

"We try to simulate the environment in the womb as closely as we can," Carole said. "So, the lights in here are always down low." She tapped a key on one of the laptop computers, and soft light from the base of the orb became a little brighter. The light illuminated a mass of skin and veins and tendrils at the bottom of the sphere. A long, vein-covered tube snaked from the bottom of the orb to a tiny baby floating in the center of the sphere.

"Oh, my God. Is he alive?"

"Very much so. And he's a she."

He marveled at her perfection. A cute, turned-up nose, thin, short hair, ten fingers and ten toes. It filled Allan with wonder. Suddenly, her eyes opened.

"She looked at me!" he shouted.

"She opens her eyes from time to time, but she can't really see," Carole said. "It's just a reflex."

"It's an incredible reflex," he said. "How old is she?"

"She's about thirty-eight weeks."

"She should be born very soon."

"I want to give her at least one more week in the tank to help her grow," Carole said.

"Damn," he said, staring back at the tiny infant in front of him. "This is the most amazing thing I have ever seen." He pulled his phone from his pocket and, turning to Carole, asked, "May I?"

She hesitated a moment. Then a confident smile crossed her lips. "Sure," she said. "Why not?" He snapped a picture.

"It is fascinating, isn't it? I could sit here and watch her for hours."

"Better than a goldfish bowl."

Carole laughed. Allan was falling for that laugh.

"How could you ever leave?"

"I seldom do. That's one of the reasons the hospital people you talked to didn't recognize my name. I spend most of my time here."

"But you left her alone from time to time."

"Rarely," Carole said. "And you'll notice I was never more than a three-minute walk from the lab. The system is connected to an app on my phone. Besides, all the baby does in there is grow. Not real traumatic, is it?"

"How long has she been, er—"

"She's been in incubation since her eighth week," Carole said.

"So, this is the third option."

"No, this is another option. But the person carrying the baby must be the one to make the choice," Carole said. "Dan's research enables us to extract the embryo at a very young age and incubate it until it is ready to survive in the world. From here, the plan would be to place the baby up for adoption."

Allan couldn't take his eyes off the little girl in the orb. "It makes so much sense. And Dan was the first to do this?"

"Actually, the concept has been around for a hundred years. It's called ectogenesis. Researchers at prominent universities have been publishing papers about this concept since the eighties."

"I take it this is the only one in existence?"

"Today it is. But I have the information we would need to duplicate this process over and over again."

"Really?"

"Yes. In about three years, we could be the McDonald's of ectogenesis."

"What about the cost? Were you able to get the costs down?"

"This prototype is very expensive. But the process doesn't have to be. We have little doubt that we could keep the costs down to a reasonable amount."

Allan's thoughts floated back to Amanda, her concerns, and his subsequent library research about adoption. "I've read that the adoption and foster care system in the States is pretty screwed up. Could it handle an influx of one hundred thousand or more children a year?"

"Well, first of all, not everyone with an unwanted pregnancy would choose ectogenesis. Some would still pick a chemical or surgical abortion. If ectogenesis were to be implemented successfully, there would need to be a lot of support at the federal level. Keep in mind, since overturning Roe, the foster care system is going to have a large influx of newborns, anyway. The question is, will people continue to be saddled with all the responsibilities of pregnancy and birth, or will they be freed from the guilt, cost and life disruption brought about by childbirth."

"Don't adopted children typically have ... mental health issues?"

"There's no doubt that adopted children face challenges that other children may not face—separation, attachment, and identity issues are common. Reactive attachment disorder is real. However, a case can be made that infant adoptions—those without the trauma from poor parenting or prolonged foster care which ectogenesis could facilitate—have fewer obstacles than those faced in the current system."

Seeing something new, for the first time, has a strange impact on the mind. It opens one to other thoughts and concepts. In this case, it caused Allan to pause and contemplate his condition. "This doesn't make sense," he said aloud.

"What?"

"If this is what Dan was working on—" he scratched the back of his head, "a way to bypass traditional methods of childbirth and present an alternative to abortion, why would anyone . . . Who would want to stop this?"

Carole replied while monitoring several computers. "That is the dilemma, isn't it? I don't know."

Allan felt that he was waking up from a dream. "It has to be someone who doesn't want this new technology out. Certainly none of the antiabortion groups would want to prevent something like this."

"Then who?" Carole asked. "People who fund abortion clinics? I seriously doubt that."

"Is there that much money in abortions?"

"No. If a physician wants to get rich, there are better ways to do so than opening an abortion clinic," Carole said, looking up from the keyboard. "When you factor in all the restrictions, fines, and threats, especially for Americans since the overturn of Roe, it's just not worth it, financially. You could make more money with a fast-food franchise."

"It just doesn't make sense."

Keith must have sat in the Prius for twenty minutes, mulling over the things he would and should say, again and again. He knew his eight-year marriage was over, even before it began. It wasn't the sex. Keith could have found ways around that, and Shelly hadn't minded at all when their lovemaking tapered off. Shelly loved LifeWatch and Dr. Joseph Strong. Her proudest day had been the day Keith started to work there. If he did anything to threaten that job, she would be devastated.

He shook his head suddenly, as if to physically dislodge the cobwebs that were distracting him. He focused his mind on the task at hand. He needed to tell Shelly about his concerns about LifeWatch. There was no easy way. He'd just have to tell her.

He stepped from his car, reached into the back seat, dragged out the old briefcase, strode up the walk to the front door, inserted the key, and entered their house.

The kitchen and family room were empty. He called upstairs, but Shelly didn't answer.

He found her out back, kneeling in the garden, pulling various weeds and debris.

"Hi, honey," she echoed back when she heard his call. "How was your day?"

"Could've been better," he said, and she returned to her weeding. She never really wanted to hear about his day, after all. Keith shifted from one foot to the other. "Shelly, we have to talk."

"So talk," she said, yanking another green stem from the wood chips.

"Please. This is important."

"It's your job again, isn't it?" she said, resting back on her haunches and placing gloved hands on the front of her thighs.

Keith sighed. "In a way, yes. Would you please hear me out?"

Irritated, Shelly stripped off the gloves and threw them on the ground. She looked up at her husband.

"Something strange is going on at LifeWatch," Keith said.

Shelly started to say something, paused as if to rethink her response, and then said, "What do you mean?"

"There are several accounts, here, there, in various departmental budgets, like IT, HR, Outreach, and so forth. Discretionary. Miscellaneous. Contingency. They're too small to be noticed, but together they add up to hundreds of thousands of dollars."

"In an organization as large as LifeWatch, I'm sure you've got lots of accounts like that."

"Yes, but these usually lie dormant. The funds roll over into the general budget at the end of the year, and they appear again in the next year's budget."

"So?"

"Just a week or so ago, they all became active. In fact, they all were emptied on about the same day."

"Okay," Shelly said. "That is odd."

"That's not all," Keith said. "They all were authorized by Joseph Strong."

"You think he's dipping into the till?"

"No, not personally." Keith pressed his palms together and rubbed them back and forth. "All the funds were transferred to a bank account held by Tom Gaines, the director of Security."

"What do you think?"

"Well, it took some maneuvering, not all of it legal, but I found that various payments were made to a former LifeWatch Security employee. And that's where the trail ends."

"Could it be for consulting work? Special security needs?"

He shook his head. "Maybe. What's interesting, though, is the timing. The money was paid out just about a week before the bombing of the abortion clinic in Atlanta."

"You don't think they're related, do you?"

"It just seems suspicious, that's all."

Shelly thought for a moment and then said, "Why don't you talk with Dr. Strong. I'm sure there's a logical explanation."

His frustration level skyrocketed. "But he authorized the payments."

"My point exactly. He can explain what the payments were for. He can clear this up."

"I tried talking to him. He blew me off."

Shelly stood up and covered his hands with hers. "Then there's nothing to worry about."

"I just don't know."

Strong felt almost frantic. High above the sprawling city of Augusta, in his fourteenth-floor office, he surveyed the city. It would be a shame to come so far only to lose it all in a debacle like this.

A knock on the door announced Tom Gaines, head of LifeWatch Security. "Ready for me, sir?"

"Yes, Tom," he said. "Come in."

The two sat in the overstuffed chairs in front of the desk. Tom sat military straight, betraying his security profession. Strong hunched over and leaned forward, as if to pounce at any possible moment. "What's the latest?" he asked.

"We've traced Sheffield's travel documents, automobile rentals, hotel stays, airplane flights, and credit card statements and have found that he is still very active."

"Where has he been?"

"Since his killing spree in the Eastern US, his travels took him to Arizona and Klaipeda, Lithuania. We assumed he was following Allan Chappel, but we have recently discovered that an obscure consultant for the Inc.Ubator office, one Dr. Carole Phillips, lives there."

"What is her situation?"

"We didn't find much on Dr. Phillips," Gaines said. "We missed her completely until Sheffield went over there. However, our intel now indicates that she may have been more involved than we knew."

"How's that?"

"There seems to be evidence that she has managed an experimental prototype laboratory for Dan Carlisle. The laws and regulations are much more lenient in former Soviet Union states."

"Do you think Chappel connected with Phillips over there?"

"Yes, sir. That is our assumption."

"Tommy, this is not good. We've got a security guard running around the world killing people, and we can't stop him? What are you doing about it?"

Tom Gaines shifted in his seat, obviously disturbed by the suggestion that he was responsible. "Sir, we are closely monitoring the situation. We are doing the best we can."

"Obviously, Tommy, your best isn't good enough." Strong sent the message home with a steely gaze.

The chief of security squirmed some more. "John Sheffield honestly believes he is stopping abortions, sir."

Strong flew into a rage. "This isn't about abortions. This has never been about abortions." Great drops of sweat burst on his forehead. "I don't give a shit about some promiscuous, pregnant whore's abortion. Hell, abortion probably keeps the crime rate down in this country by keeping the criminals out of the gene pool."

Gaines remained as straight as a board, eyes on Joseph Strong.

Strong paused a moment. Knowing he had stepped over the line, he added, "Tom, this fiasco may sink our entire enterprise. We have to stop this lunatic, now!"

"Yes, sir," Tom Gaines replied. "Rest assured that I will do everything within my power to stop him."

A confident smile graced Strong's face. "I know you will. You're a good man."

———————————

Allan could have watched the baby in the glass bubble for hours. It mesmerized him.

As he stared at her, he recalled a late-night apartment debate at Emory during his seminary days.

"You're full of shit," Ronnie Marshall shouted, sloshing a mug half full of beer in the direction of the short-haired and thin-skinned guy sitting in the recliner across the coffee table from him.

Kevin Price, who had a diet soda can tucked between his legs, held his hands up to shield himself. "Easy, man. My wife will kill me if I come home smelling like a brewery."

"It would probably be the first time," Ronnie muttered.

Philosophical debate was a part of every student's collegiate experience. The best debates took place in dorm rooms and apartments late at night. In seminary, debates weren't just verbal fights. They were more like professional wrestling matches with words. In grandiose fashion, seminary students would quote Kant, Kierkegaard, and Kafka as if they knew what they were talking about. When people got desperate, they would even channel the spirit of Friedrich Nietzsche to win a debate.

At 1:30 in the morning, five seminarians lay scattered about Allan's apartment like rag dolls strewn about a kindergarten room. That night, they chose a heated topic. Ronnie took the pro-choice argument, and Kevin predictably took the pro-life argument.

"The real issue is very simple," Kevin said. "At what point is the child alive? If it's alive, then aborting it is murder. End of debate."

"Can a six-week-old embryo exist outside of the womb?" Ronnie challenged. "I think not. Therefore, it is not alive, and abortion is not 'murder,' as you say." He emphasized the word using an eerie voice, like a radio spook show from the 1930s.

Kevin countered, "A six-week-old fetus has a heartbeat! It's alive, darn it!" Kevin never cussed.

"It's not even called a fetus until week ten, man. Get your facts straight."

"Who cares what it's called. It's still alive."

"At ten weeks, it looks like a lima bean," Ronnie pointed out.

"Who cares what it looks like," Kevin said. "It has arms, legs, fingers, toes, eyes. It is alive, and to kill it is murder."

"You've got fingers and toes," Ronnie said. "We could debate whether you're really alive or brain dead."

"Conception, Ronnie. After conception, halting the growth is murder."

Allan looked around the room at the other two seminarians. One was asleep in a beanbag chair. The other quietly observed the verbal match. Allan held a great deal of respect for David Sparks, an exceptional student who generally tolerated differences in opinion and always knew his stuff. He only stepped into a debate after he had done his research and knew all of the issues.

"You're kinda quiet, Sparks," Allan remarked. "What do you think?"

David looked his way with a knowing expression on his face. Allan loved that look. Somebody was about to get schooled.

"I think you're asking the wrong question," he said.

All eyes, except those of the sleeping seminarian, were on David.

"The question isn't when life begins. That doesn't matter. A cow has life, but we kill it for hamburgers. A tree has life, but we kill it for wood to build our homes. When life begins isn't the issue."

"So you're one of those pro-choice idiots who thinks any inconvenience to a woman is a valid excuse to kill a baby, right?" Kevin asked.

"Wrong," David said. "I'm a minister, and a theologian. The important thing to me is the soul, and the only question to ask is, 'When does the soul exist?'"

"What are you rambling about?" Kevin asked. The first-year seminarian didn't know David Sparks very well.

"Sparks doesn't ramble," Allan said, enjoying the game.

David Sparks took a sip of beer from his mug. "Consider this. In early Jewish law, the fetus is thought of as a part of its mother, and not a full-fledged human, until its head emerges from the womb. Exodus 21 describes a situation in which a pregnant woman miscarries because she is struck by two men fighting. The guilty party was required to pay a monetary fine, instead of being put to death, which would have been the penalty if the guilty party actually killed another human being."

Both of the younger students had bewildered looks on their faces.

"In fact, Numbers 5 even cites a recipe of sorts to cause a miscarriage if a wife has been unfaithful. Heck, guys. Go back to the second chapter of Genesis and tell me when the man became alive—it was when God had breathed in the 'breath of life.'"

One of the newbies grabbed a pocket Bible and scanned the front of the book.

"Some cited the concept of doubtful viability to dictate when one who takes a child's life would be punished with death. It stated that an embryo is still an embryo until a certain point in time—some said thirty days after its birth, when it became a bar kayyama, a viable and living creature," Sparks said. "So, when is it that a body obtains a soul: at conception, at birth, or after the birth?"

Allan and David knew the issues were much more complex than the simple conversation could cover, but it was fun to watch seminary rookies struggle with new concepts. He remembered thinking, *One way to kill a party is to raise a question that no one can answer.* Everybody, even the guy sleeping in the corner, left soon after.

Allan studied the little girl in the glass bubble in front of him. "What about it, honey? Do you have a soul?"

TWELVE

That afternoon, Carole and Allan ran a few errands. She needed some items from the local "IKI" grocery store. Before shopping, however, Carole took Allan to a business located on an upper floor of one of the buildings in the newer section of the city.

They entered the office, and she spoke with the receptionist in Lithuanian. At one point, she nodded to Allan, and he smiled and nodded back.

They moved past the receptionist's desk and into a back room. A lady came from one of the offices and gave Carole a huge welcoming hug. Again, Carole said something and nodded toward Allan.

"Allan, this is Evgenia Kripinevich, the director." He stepped forward, nodded, and shook her hand.

They chatted a bit more and then Carole led him back to a conference room.

"This is an adoption agency," she said. "Evgenia specializes in infant adoptions."

"Oh."

Carole turned on the light, and Allan was instantly greeted by framed photographs of dozens of babies' faces covering the conference room walls. "These are the children that this agency has placed. And these," Carole said, walking around the room and touching pictures here and there, high and low, "are children I birthed using our process."

"Really? I thought the baby in the lab was the first."

"No. She is the only one in process now. But she will be number seven when she is born."

"You've birthed six babies using this method?"

"Shhhh. Don't raise your voice," Carole placed her finger over her lips. "Evgenia thinks I operate a home for unwed mothers."

Carole gazed at one of the photos for a long time and seemed to change her mind. "On the other hand, I don't think Evgenia would mind. In fact, I think she'd welcome any practice if it helped a baby survive. She loves her foster children."

"Have any failed?" Allan asked

A solemn look crossed her face. "Yes. Two, a couple of years ago. But you know, over thirty percent of pregnancies end in miscarriage, so I believe we are ahead of the curve." He admired her optimism.

Allan paused for a moment. "It occurred to me there may be other opportunities for your ectogenesis process."

"Yes?"

"It sounds like you're suggesting it might be used to reduce abortions, but it might also be a way to save people whose lives are endangered by being pregnant."

"Yes, Dan and I discussed that," Carole said, studying one of the photos.

"Some people get abortions so they don't have to endure the stress of pregnancy. Your ectogenesis process could provide another option for those people."

"It's possible this process would be worth millions to anyone who developed it, but Dan didn't seem interested in the money. He was just focused on reducing abortions... though I don't really know why."

Allan thought he knew what was behind Dan's concern with abortion.

"At any rate, until we receive legal consent, we'll have to be content with the system we have," she said.

They went to the post office, and Carole mailed some bills. Then they went to a nearby IKI grocery store. She made her purchases, and he helped her carry the bags to her apartment.

Carole had work to do, so Allan dismissed himself and headed back to the guesthouse. His head swam with the overwhelming information he'd learned that day about the progress Carole and Dan had made on this radical new process. Unwed mothers, teenagers, and people suffering from illness or poverty would all have an alternative to abortion or birth. The world was about to change, again.

Deep in thought, he almost didn't notice the police officers in the lobby. He saw them, dressed in trim dark blue uniforms without caps, at the last moment, through the window on the front door as he reached to open it. He released the door handle fast, as if it were scalding hot. With his back pressed against the brick wall, he took a few breaths, looked around to see if anyone had noticed, then put his head down and walked past the guesthouse.

It took every ounce of will to walk on, heart pounding, as if nothing was out of the ordinary. At the next block, he turned right, out of sight of the guesthouse, and ran. He sprinted up the cobblestone street, down a side alley and past homes and office buildings, stopping to catch his breath in a little park filled with Soviet-style statues. Beyond the park, a Russian Orthodox church stood in the distance, a reminder of beliefs, cultures, and views foreign to him.

He slumped down on a granite park bench and searched his mind. What had he left behind? He had left some clothes, a phone charger, and some toiletries. Had he left anything that might implicate Carole? No. He breathed a bit easier. But only a bit.

He went back to Carole's. It was the only place he could go. He took a roundabout route, checking again and again to make sure no one was following him. Ducking into a little café, he watched the street through the plate glass window. When he was sure no one was following, he found his way to her apartment and the lab.

He tapped on the outside door. Carole opened it a few moments later.

"What happened?"

"When I got back to the guesthouse, the Klaipeda police were there. I'm sure they were looking for me."

"Oh, no. Were you followed?" She peered up and down the tiny street.

"No. I don't think they saw me."

"Quickly, come inside."

They entered the dark hall, and Carole turned to face him. The hallway was tight and cozy. "You'll have to stay here. I have a sofa. It's as uncomfortable as hell, but it's the best I can offer."

"I'll take anything."

She led him up a flight of concrete steps to the second floor. Her keys jangled as she unlocked the door. He stepped into one of the warmest homes he'd ever entered. Hardwood floors were partially covered with large ornate rugs. Paintings of children and Lithuanian scenery hung from the walls. A spotless counter separated the living room from the kitchenette.

He walked over to the sofa, touched it as if to give it some sort of comfort test and said, "This will be perfect. When we figure out what to do next, I'll leave."

"You're welcome to stay as long as necessary," she said. "Let me get something for the sofa." She brought a blanket and sheets from a back room, which he assumed was her bedroom, and placed them on the edge of the couch.

"I need to go downstairs and double-check the project," she said. "I wanted to cook dinner for us tonight. I'll be thirty minutes or so, and then we can prepare it together, okay?"

"Perfect," he said.

She slipped out the front door, and he slumped back into the sofa. Something in the back of his mind gnawed at him. While she wasn't perfect, Aunt Julia usually warned him of danger. Why hadn't she told him the police were going to be at the guesthouse? He pulled his phone from his pocket and checked for text messages but found none. He dialed her number. The phone rang four times and then went to voicemail. He chose not to leave a message.

He settled back into the sofa and let his mind slow down to rest.

Dr. Joseph P. Strong stood before the large plate glass window and surveyed the sprawling city of Augusta before him. From this vantage point, he could see thousands of houses, buildings, schools, offices, and church steeples and miles of roadways. He loved this view. He loved this city.

But the time had come to move on. The next steps in this grand experience called life beckoned. It was time to connect with his destiny. Destiny is hard to ignore. Like a seductress, she calls to her lover, and he must respond.

Well, Dr. Joseph P. Strong was ready to respond. He knew his destiny. She would take him places his poor mama and daddy never could. She had called him to Washington, into politics and away from his past commitments.

To be sure, he had played his part in following her. He had taken steps that many would have questioned, and most would have called immoral and illegal, but that could only be understood in terms of the end results.

The glint of sunlight on a church steeple caught his eye and reminded him that he would miss Augusta, with its sleepy businesses and cozy comforts.

The phone on the desk behind him buzzed lightly. "Joseph?" his receptionist asked. She was one of the only people in the organization who called him by his first name. "I have Reverend Williams on line one. He wants to know if you'll join him for the antiabortion protest next month."

He clenched his fists in anger. He didn't have time to talk about stupid protests. He didn't care about abortions or the soulless sluts who had them. He had more important things that demanded his time and attention.

But then, the pro-life group and their deep pockets had enabled him to get this far, and they were about to take him forward.

"Kindly reassure the good reverend that I look forward to joining him next month, dear," he said.

Strong had learned long ago that abortion, or opposing it, was a cash cow for many politicians. If abortion were to become illegal nationwide, or if it were to become obsolete, as that stupid Carlisle procedure had threatened, he would have a difficult time finding an issue as emotionally charged to fund his multimillion-dollar election campaigns.

But the Carlisle process was not much of a threat anymore. It would probably take five more years before another enterprising young doctor would attempt to intervene. By then, Joseph P. Strong would be comfortably started in his second term in office. Then they could do whatever they wanted.

"Reverend Williams would like to talk with you about the abortion clinic bombing," the receptionist called through the intercom.

Destiny, his elusive seductress, was still waiting. He would need help to reach her.

He picked up the phone. "Reverend Williams! How marvelous it is to talk with you," he said.

Allan needed a plan. He knew it, and so did Carole.

"They're getting closer," he said over a dish of pasta. "Either the police or the bald man will catch up with me eventually."

"What are you going to do?" she asked.

"I don't know." He wished she had asked what they were going to do.

"They will find you," she said. "Some police officer will recognize your face in the IKI or in the mall, and they'll take you to jail."

She was right. It was only a matter of time. "I could go back and face the music," he said. "Hire an attorney, show pictures of what you're doing here. Prove that I had nothing to do with the bombing."

"That could be very risky. It may not work."

"Besides, I don't know if I could get back to the States. By now they're on to the fact that I'm using Wes's passport."

"I might be able to help with that," she said.

"What do you mean?"

"You know, none of the babies that we've delivered have valid birth certificates. After all, their mothers don't really know that their fetuses survived. They thought they came for an abortion."

The word struck a nerve. "I didn't know that."

"It was the only way we could keep our operation secret and still be able to prove it worked."

"How can this help me?"

"I work with a very skilled artist. He makes birth certificates for all of the children we incubate. We pay him well, but it's worth every euro."

"Could he make a passport for me?"

"Sure. For a price," she said.

"I don't have much money."

"Don't worry. The funds from the Inc.Ubator organization will be sufficient."

"So, if I were to get back to America, is there anything I can take back to prove the process works? I feel like the only way I can show my innocence is by demonstrating that the process works and that I wasn't some mad antiabortionist."

"I've got photos, videos, and all the documentation you might need," she said.

"Is it safe? You know, they destroyed the office in Atlanta."

"It's backed up on servers all over the world," she said. "I can share digital copies with you."

He sighed, resolved. "Well, then, it looks like I need to go back."

"It won't be easy," she told him.

"It's the only way. Will you be safe?" he asked.

"I think so. The police are chasing you for crimes committed in the United States. They have no reason to suspect me of anything," she said.

"After I'm gone," Allan added, "I'm concerned that the bald man may come after you." He took her hand in his own.

"I doubt that he will. He's here for you, so I imagine he'll follow you back across the Atlantic," Carole said, with a little less than confidence in her voice.

"Why don't you come back with me?" Allan asked. He hoped the suggestion sounded platonic, but he wished for more.

"I can't leave my work," she said. "Besides, I'm not well known here. I doubt that he will be able to find me."

"I pray to God he doesn't."

———————————

Allan woke in the dark. Someone was in the room.

He never had been a heavy sleeper, but these days, he barely closed his eyes. It may have been the creak of the floor or the soft breathing, but he knew someone was there.

She touched a soft fingertip to his lips. "Shhh."

He started to sit up, but she gently pressed him back onto the sofa.

Her finger was soon replaced with her soft lips, which parted slightly when his tongue reached out to welcome them. Her kisses became more passionate as he pressed on. When he placed his hand on her naked breast, she gasped.

She pushed aside the blanket and crawled on top of him. They continued to kiss, their lips locked together as their hands explored each other's bodies. She pulled him into her and began to rock back and forth. The creaking of the sofa echoed the rhythm of her soft sounds. Both rose in volume and intensity.

Once again, Allan knew his life would never be the same.

THIRTEEN

There are things you do at work that are covered in a formal job description stored on some hard drive in HR. There are things you do at work because you are asked, even if they aren't a part of the job. Then, there are things you do, which you know you shouldn't, because you have no choice.

Keith had only been on the job for three months when Dr. Strong surprised him one morning at his cubicle. "Keith Edwards?" he asked.

"Uh, yes, sir."

"I wondered if you could help me out this morning," Dr. Strong said. "I've cleared it with your boss. Got a moment?"

"Yes, sir," Keith said, standing beside his desk.

Strong had already started walking away. Keith searched his desk, grabbed a pen and notepad, and started after the CEO of LifeWatch. His pulse raced as he wondered what Dr. Joseph P. Strong might want from him, a newbie accountant.

Dr. Strong's office was as nice as Keith could have imagined. Keith sat in one of the padded chairs opposite Dr. Strong's massive desk, waiting while the CEO washed his hands in his private bathroom. The cherry wood of the surrounding furniture and the ornate wood molding on the walls gave the room an exquisite feel. Keith's Goodwill suit and discount store shoes didn't seem to belong here.

"Thank you for joining me, Keith," Dr. Strong said. He wiped his hands on a small towel as he exited his personal bathroom. "How are you today?"

"I'm fine, sir," Keith answered.

Dr. Strong settled his fit frame into his oversized office chair and leaned forward on his elbows. "Keith, I need your help. Before I ask, I need to know that I can count on your support and your confidentiality."

"Of course, sir."

The CEO scrutinized Keith's eyes, as if trying to discern whether he was telling the truth. "Good, then."

He reached into his upper desk drawer, retrieved a white envelope, and handed it to Keith. "There's an address on the outside of that envelope. I need you to take the envelope to that address this morning at ten o'clock. A blond-haired lady will be waiting for you. She goes by the name of Helen. Give her that envelope and—now, this is important—make sure she goes inside the business at that address. Wait for ten minutes to ensure that she doesn't just come back out. Is that clear?" He pointed his finger across the desk for emphasis.

"Yes, sir. I understand."

"You're a good man, Keith."

"Thank you, sir."

He arrived at the street address five minutes before ten o'clock. A blonde, wearing a short denim skirt and a low-cut, tattered, and stained blouse stood in front of the doors to the family planning clinic.

"Are you Helen?"

"Yeah. You got it?" She puffed on a Winston.

Keith handed over the envelope. She didn't look inside but stuffed it in a ragged purse hanging from her shoulder and turned to walk away.

"Wait a minute," Joseph said. "You're supposed to go inside."

"I will. I've just gotta take care of something first."

"No. They told me you would have to go inside immediately, or I have to call the cops." He pulled his phone from his pocket. He was improvising, and it seemed to be working.

The blonde paused a moment, as if unsure of what to do. She scratched her forearm. Finally, she stomped her feet in frustration. "Shit. All right, motherfuckin' Boy Scout." She pushed through the doors to the clinic and disappeared inside.

Keith waited in his car for ten minutes, as he had been told. Helen did not come out.

He turned on the ignition, took one last look at the clinic doors, and drove away.

––––––––––––––––––

Breakfast tasted better than ever to Allan that morning. Carole kissed him warmly and went downstairs to work. He volunteered to go to IKI for some groceries.

"Be careful," she told him. "Watch your back."

He bundled up and prepared to walk the four blocks to the grocery store. Suddenly, his phone pinged, alerting him to an incoming text message. He raised it and read the text from Aunt Julia's phone: *Hope all is well. I am doing fine. Sunny here in Arizona. Where are you?*

Allan didn't know what made him pause. Maybe it was his own psychic sense, or the fact that Aunt Julia seemed much more talkative in this text, or that he hadn't heard from her when the police appeared at the guesthouse the day before, but something made him feel uneasy about this message. He turned the phone off and stuffed it in his pocket, but he couldn't stop thinking about the text. Pulling his gloves and coat on, he ventured out the front door into the cold Klaipeda weather.

He pondered the message all the way down the street. Aunt Julia never asked about his location. It just wasn't her way. If she needed him, she used to say, the stars would bring them together. She also never mentioned her own well-being. Hoping he was well seemed way out of the ordinary. Confident in her own abilities, she always knew if he was well or not.

Once inside the IKI, Allan tugged his gloves off and stuffed them in his jacket pocket. Grabbing a basket, he began to select items on the shopping list Carole had written earlier that morning. These stores were small in comparison to the grocery stores back home. Still, they managed to carry quite a variety of items.

Halfway down the second aisle, he thought he might give Aunt Julia a call, just to see if everything was okay. He turned on his phone and listened as it rang.

The small store was fairly empty that morning but still full of sounds. The IKI's own musical jingle played now and then. Someone loading something in the back of the store dropped cartons of items with a ka-klunk. The heater fan blew from a device suspended from the ceiling.

But, slipping through the noise, he heard something else. A cell phone rang. Allan felt certain it had started ringing when he dialed Aunt Julia's number.

Since she didn't answer, he hung up. The ringing of the other phone stopped as well.

A tightening began in his stomach. He felt his pulse beat harder in his neck. The idea that someone with Aunt Julia's phone might be here, in Klaipeda, in this IKI, made him break out in a cold sweat.

He dialed the number again, and again a phone, several aisles over, rang.

He hung up his phone again and ducked behind a stack of canned vegetables. He chanced a look around the corner of the display. An old lady, toddling along behind a small cart, was the only person in sight.

He felt himself breathe easier. Then he glanced up into one corner of the room and saw a large, round mirror. In its reflection, he could make out a lone figure, distorted by the oval mirror's shape. The man wore a heavy black coat and a dark cap. Allan couldn't see his face. He had to get closer.

Windows of plate glass lined the front of the store. He thought he might get a better glimpse of the big guy through the reflection. He slipped around the corner to the next aisle. He was just two or three aisles away, but he still couldn't see the reflection clearly in the window. It was too bright outside.

Allan slipped around the corner of the next aisle, but the view wasn't any clearer. He started to the next display and ran into the old lady with the shopping cart.

"Oje!" she exclaimed, and Allan jumped back.

He felt exposed now. He had lost track of the man in the overcoat. He cautiously moved toward the end of the display, aware that his movements looked extremely odd but fearing he might get caught. He looked around the corner of the display and saw a figure standing about twenty feet away, with his back toward Allan. He seemed to be trying to read the labels on some wine bottles. Allan still couldn't see his face.

Directly behind him was a fish display. The grocer who took fish orders had left the counter. Allan dashed across the aisle, in full sight, had the guy turned to look his way. He pushed through some swinging doors into the stocking area. It was empty.

Turning left, he crept up to the fish counter.

He could see the man now, with his back to Allan. He looked for mirrors in the store, but none were in a position to reveal the man's face. Allan had to know if it was the bald man.

He pulled out his phone again and started to dial Aunt Julia's number. His breath came in puffs in the frigid stocking area of the store. If it was the bald man and his phone rang when Allan dialed her number, he would know the bald man had Aunt Julia's phone and was here in Lithuania. He took another look in the big man's direction. The man was no longer looking at the wine bottles but was scrutinizing something in his hands.

Before he could press the dial button, Allan felt his phone vibrate and chime in his hands. He backed up, trying to silence the device. It dropped to the concrete floor. He grabbed it in time to silence it on the fifth note.

"Hello?" the bald man in the heavy black coat called in his direction. "Hello?" He inched closer to the fish counter.

Allan fell to the floor and rolled under a sink packed with ice and fish. The concrete was icy cold, and water was leaking slowly from a pipefitting.

Inches away, and separated by a tin wall, Allan's enemy stood silently waiting. Allan held his breath. He felt the man's presence—an evil, ominous presence—on the other side. Several frozen moments later, he heard him shuffle on down the aisle.

Rolling out from beneath the sink, Allan rose into a crouch and moved farther back into the stockroom. Finding a back door, he shoved it open and ran into the light. Down one alley, left at the next. He ran as fast as he could, not even looking back to see if his foe followed. He eventually decided he had, once again, eluded the bald man. He hailed a cab on H. Manto Gatve, one of the main streets, and rode back to Carole's apartment, watching through the back windows to ensure he was alone.

———————————

He entered her apartment like a tornado, throwing his coat on the sofa and heading for the kitchen. He searched for something to drink, found a small bottle of cognac, and emptied it into a glass. The warm liquid felt like fire in his cold belly.

He sat down at the kitchen table to think.

"Hello! I thought I heard footsteps up here." Carole came through the front door. "I made arrangements with the man who creates our birth certificates. We should be able to pick up the passport this afternoon," she said. Then, focusing on Allan, she said, "What's wrong?"

He looked up from the glass and took a deep breath. "He's here."

"Who?"

"The bald man who's chasing me."

Carole pulled out the chair opposite him. "How can that be?"

"I don't know. Maybe he traced Wes's passport. I saw him in the IKI."

"You must have been mistaken," she said.

"I know he's here. He even had my aunt's cell phone. I dialed her number twice, and the phone he held rang at the same time. Then, when he pressed some keys, I got a text message from her phone." He showed her his broken phone. Even through the cracks in the glass, he could read the text message that said, *Allan. Did you try to call me?*

Her look of uncertainty changed to one of fear. Her hands moved up to her mouth, as if she were protecting herself with her arms. "But how—"

Allan took another gulp of cognac and shook his head.

"Your cell phone, Allan. Does it have a GPS?"

"Don't they all?"

"I read somewhere that hackers can track people using the GPS in their phones, even when the phones aren't turned on," she said.

"Oh, my God." He yanked the phone from the table and opened the little drawer on the side. He pulled out the SIM card. Then, he got up from the table, found a meat mallet in the kitchen, and proceeded to pound the phone until it was nothing more than a few pieces on the countertop.

"Oh, dear God," Carole whispered.

"Don't worry. I won't let him get to you."

"Right now," she said, staring at the mallet, "I'm more frightened of you."

He tossed the hammer onto the countertop, a bit harder than he should have. It slid across the counter and hit a framed picture that had been leaning against the kitchen wall. He quickly reached for it, afraid that he had broken that glass as well.

The photograph was of several people posing side by side in an office. Most of the faces in the photograph looked vaguely familiar. Dan Carlisle was in the front row with his arm around Carole's shoulder. Another woman stood next to him. The back row contained several other people that Allan did not recognize, except for the man standing in the back at the end of the row. He had a high forehead with short, patchy hair. His chin was bare. But his beefy face and the crooked, broken nose were unmistakable.

"When was this picture taken?" he asked Carole.

"A year or so ago, when I visited the States."

"Do you know this man in the corner?" he asked, pointing to him.

"Who?" She squinted at the photograph. "Not really. I think he was in charge of security. I don't remember his name."

"Are you sure?" He pounded the table.

"Allan, calm down."

"Don't tell me to calm down. The guy in this photo tried to kill me on at least two occasions. I don't think he's going to stop now."

She accepted the photo with trembling hands. "Yes. He did something with security. Are you sure he's the same man?"

"I've seen him up close and personal. He's the guy."

Carole's fingers continued to tremble. She grasped the counter for support.

He sat back in the wooden chair. "He's here in this city. It's only a matter of time before he finds us, if he hasn't already."

His mind began to race. Maybe Carole knew this guy better than she had admitted. He stood up and leaned forward with his hands on the table.

"Do you know him?"

"No, Allan."

"Carole?"

"I did not know him."

"How can I trust you?"

"You have to."

Fear and anger mingled in his mind. "Why?" He slapped the countertop with his hand. The sound echoed throughout the small apartment.

"Because I'm all you have," she said.

Her words stopped him like a brick wall. She was right. He had nothing and no one else. She was all he had. He slumped away from the wall and back into the wooden chair.

They both were silent for a long time.

"May I borrow your phone?" Allan asked.

She went to her purse and brought it to him.

He racked his brain and recalled the number for Gus Jacoby. Gus had lived next door to Aunt Julia for years. A while back, his wife had died, and Allan always suspected that he and Aunt Julia would occasionally gather together for more than just bridge.

The phone rang three times before he picked it up. "Mr. Jacoby? This is Allan Chappel, Julia's nephew."

"Oh, hello, Allan. Have you talked with Julie?"

Julie? Allan thought. "No," he responded. "I can't reach her. Is everything all right?"

"Oh, my, son," he said. "She was attacked. Robbed, she was, in broad daylight, or dusk, at least." Allan held his breath.

"She's at Arrowhead Community Hospital," Gus said. "I just came from there, and she is in stable condition."

"I'm so glad to hear that, Mr. Jacoby."

"It was touch and go there for a bit, let me tell you. The guy who attacked her took her purse, and she didn't have more than twenty dollars in it. Damn this world. What's next?"

"Tell her that I'm thinking of her when you see her again," Allan said.

"That'll be tomorrow."

"Tell her that I'm okay. Make sure she rests."

"Will do," he said. "Are you planning to visit anytime soon?"

"As soon as I am able."

"Very well. I'll let you go."

"Thanks again, Mr. Jacoby. I appreciate all of your help."

After he hung up, Allan pondered their situation and the woman he was with. She was no longer safe, even if Allan went back home. "You need to come with me."

"To the States? I can't."

"Why not?"

"The baby isn't ready," she said. "I can't leave here until we extract her."

"He is going to kill us," Allan said, slowly, word by word.

"I'll have to take that chance," she said. "I can't risk it."

He felt exasperated. "Remind me how far along she is."

"She's in her thirty-eighth week. We've never birthed a baby until week forty."

"We have to leave. Can you speed up the growth process?"

"No. She can't be rushed."

"Then we have to leave her behind," he said.

"I will not!" She looked at him with steely eyes, determined to see this through.

"Carole," he said, as convincingly as possible. "We have to extract her early, now. The three of us will go to the United States together. We can leave as soon as you are ready."

She took a deep breath. "We have so much to do."

They went downstairs to the lab, and Carole began to detail what they needed to do. She checked the calendar three times. She studied the baby closely and noted changes that might indicate a readiness to be birthed. She took a syringe and extracted some liquid from a small vial, then inserted the liquid into a tube that led into the base beneath the glass orb. "This will help prepare the baby for extraction," she said. "We can't go back now. We must deliver this child."

"How long does this take?" Allan asked.

"About four or five hours," she said. "Unlike a normal pregnancy, we don't have to worry about the mother's readiness. We just focus on the child."

She gave him a list of things she needed for the trip. "Hurry, please, Allan. I may need your help here in a couple of hours."

He left the basement, concerned about the child, excited about the future, and scared of what might be waiting out in the street.

FOURTEEN

Allan returned from his errands late in the afternoon. He'd purchased a couple of knapsacks, lots of baby care stuff, some comfortable clothes, and a new cell phone. He also bought a couple of door alarms from a security store.

Although he considered it, he didn't buy a gun. He didn't speak Lithuanian and did not want to draw too much attention to himself, which he probably would if he tried to purchase a pistol. Also, he knew nothing about guns and expected that he would probably shoot himself in the ass before he shot the bald man.

He met Carole's artist friend and picked up the birth certificate and passport. Both looked impeccable. Earlier, on his way to the grocery store, he had dropped in on the artist and made a couple of special requests. He hoped Carole would like them.

Leaving his purchases at Carole's apartment, he went downstairs to see how she was doing with the baby. He set the motion detector alarms on the basement and apartment doors.

"You're just in time," she said. "You are about to witness the birth of baby number seven, using the Carlisle technique."

"I have to tell you something first," he said.

"Make it snappy," Carole said.

"I named the baby."

"What?"

"You chose the name 'Irina Voznaja.' That was okay, but I talked to your artist friend and asked him to change it."

"And?"

"Meet 'Amber Carole Phillips,'" he said proudly, pointing to the baby girl in the glass bowl.

"Amber! I love it!" Carole said.

"I also changed my name," he said, holding out his passport, which displayed his new name: Allan Phillips. "Now we can travel as a family."

"Okay. That might make it more convenient." She seemed a little hesitant about that name change.

"So," he said. "You do like the name 'Amber Phillips,' don't you?"

"It's a great choice."

"I even bought her a teething bracelet in the park. It's made of amber," he said, even more proudly.

"You didn't! Not in the park."

"Why? Are they dirty? We can clean it."

"No, you probably can't."

"What do you mean?"

Carole shook her head and said, "Go get it."

He obediently went upstairs and fetched all of the baby items he had purchased that day. Reluctantly, he handed over the teething bracelet.

"You bought this in the park, right?" she asked.

"Yes. Two or three women were selling lots of amber jewelry from makeshift tables today. The prices were really good."

"I'll bet they were." She took the bracelet and rubbed one of the stones against her jeans. She sniffed that stone closely and placed it in her mouth. "Just as I thought. Taste."

He held the bracelet to his lips and licked one of the stones. It tasted sweet.

"Allan," Carole said. "It's toffee. It's a popular scam with the vendors in the park. They fool tourists into thinking they're getting a great price on real amber jewelry, but they're actually selling jewelry made of toffee." He felt like an idiot.

Carole seemed to sense his dejected feelings, and she came over and hugged him. Wrapping slender arms around his waist, she said, "But it was a very sweet gesture." She started laughing.

He laughed also. They laughed at each other and could barely contain themselves.

She squeezed him tighter. "We're going to get out of this, aren't we?"

"You, me, and Baby Amber," he said. "The sweetest baby in the world." They both started laughing again.

"All right," Carole said. "Stop fooling around and help me birth this baby."

Allan stopped laughing. "Where do we start?"

"First, we need to wash up," she replied. They used surgical soap at the sink and donned sterile gowns.

Carole led Allan to the glass globe and told him to remove the drape. When he did so, he noticed the top of the sphere consisted of a lid and gasket that was sealed into place. At her instruction, he reached up and began to release the lid. He removed it and set it on the table beside the sphere.

"We're going to need more sterile towels," she said, so he went back to the sink and grabbed a stack of blue and white ones.

An ear-piercing sound ripped his focus away from the towels and Carole and the baby, toward the hallway outside. The front door burst open beside him and the tiny alarm he had set earlier screamed as if it had been wounded.

The bald man rushed inside and quickly surveyed the lab. In the dim light, Allan could see the glistening metal of a pistol in his hand.

When the invader's eyes fell on the glass sphere with the baby inside, softly lit by lighting in the base, his face twisted into a knot of intense anger. "What have you done, you evil freaks?" he shouted. He raised his pistol and pointed it at the glass orb.

Leaping at the man's arm with all his strength, Allan managed to catch it just before the pistol went off, causing the bullet to miss the target by several inches and crash into something at the back of the lab. As he grabbed at the pistol hand, Allan's fingers became entwined in the man's wristwatch, and the flimsy band broke, sending the watch sliding across the room toward Carole.

The bald man shook Allan off his arm like a dog might shake a toy and turned to pistol whip him. Allan managed to kick his legs toward the big guy's feet and sideswiped his legs. The man slipped and fell to the floor, discharging the gun again. Something else splintered in the back of the room.

Allan took a quick glance and saw Carole reaching into the sphere through the open space at the top and gently pulling the baby from the liquid. She turned her back as if to shield the child with her body, should the bald man fire again.

He searched for the bald man and saw him lying on the floor, raising the pistol in Carole's direction. Allan dove for the gun, but this time the invader anticipated his move and stiff-armed him with his free hand. Allan still managed to hit his body hard enough that the third shot went wild.

"I finally caught you, you goddamn, slippery bastard," the man yelled as he swung and hit Allan with the butt of his pistol. Bursts of white light flashed through Allan's eyes and for a moment he couldn't see. He had to get that gun. He had to stop him.

The bald man rose to one knee and again pointed the gun toward Carole and the baby she protected with her body. Allan leapt toward him and knocked him off balance again. They rolled beneath a table and its wooden legs buckled from the force. The table—books, equipment, and all—tumbled down on top of them.

Allan couldn't breathe. The force of the falling table had knocked the wind out of him. Try as he might, he couldn't pull air into his lungs. He felt his chest begin to tighten and wondered if he would breathe in again or pass out.

The bald man was pulling himself out from beneath the debris. As if in slow motion, he half crawled toward the gun that had slid into the corner. Carole and the baby were hiding somewhere on the other side of the room.

Allan had to stop the bald man. He forced himself up into a push-up position. The table rose with him. He rolled to his left, and the tabletop fell behind him. As he pulled himself into a crouch, his hand fell on one of the table legs. He charged the bald man, dragging the hunk of wood like a baseball bat.

The big guy turned the gun toward Allan just as he swung. It was a lucky hit. The gun went flying like a line drive toward the wall. Allan heard the bald man scream when the table leg tore into his beefy hand. The makeshift bat slipped from Allan's fingers and tumbled toward the glass orb in the middle of the room.

The bald man cocked his bloody hand back and released it with incredible force toward Allan's face. It met its mark and Allan tumbled backwards to the floor. The man followed after him. He reached for Allan with both hands, squeezing his throat with thick, muscular fingers. He forced his weight on Allan's throat as he knelt over the smaller man. Huge globs of sweat and blood and drool dripped from his open mouth and fell on Allan's face. The eagle tattoo peeked out from beneath the bald man's open collar. Allan tried hitting him. He tried to wriggle away. He could not escape.

He felt the oxygen drain from his lungs. He struggled to breathe, twisting his head from side to side and bucking his body. The lab began to grow dark, and he heard the loud incessant screaming of the child Carole had just pulled from the incubator orb and the high-pitched wail of the activated door alarm. Knowing the bald man literally held his life in his hands, Allan felt an odd feeling of peace. He stopped struggling and allowed his mind to turn to Carole and Amber. He willed them to escape. *Run. Run away. Now.* It was all he could do.

When the bald man had burst through the laboratory doors, Carole went into protection mode. She reached inside the glass orb shirt sleeves and all— damn the sterile procedures—and pulled the child from the viscous liquid. She dragged the helpless infant to her breast and attempted to extract the veiny umbilical cord, which was connected to the artificial placenta still floating in the tank. She flinched when she heard a gunshot, followed by shattering wood on the other side of the laboratory. Across the room, a table fell with a loud crash as Allan and the bald man struggled with the pistol. Scissors! She needed scissors to cut the baby's cord. She spied them on a counter several feet away.

She stretched as far as the baby's umbilical cord would allow her but still could not reach them. A piece of wood—a table leg?—fell against her foot. She looked up and saw the bald man lying on top of Allan's body, his hands wrapped tightly around Allan's throat. She had to help Allan, or the bald man would kill them all. Reaching into the glass orb, she grabbed the artificial placenta and ripped it from its restraints. Carrying the screaming baby in the crook of her left arm while the artificial placenta bounced against her leg, she reached down, grabbed the table leg at her feet, and turned to the front of the laboratory where the two men were struggling. She took two long strides and swung the club at the bald man's hairless melon, sending him sprawling across the floor. He wasn't dead, but he would have a hell of a headache when he woke up.

Carole dropped the wooden weapon and cuddled the crying bundle of life in her arms. Allan stood on shaky legs and reached for her.

"Scissors," she said.

He found the scissors and other surgical supplies on the counter near the glass sphere. The floor was slick with liquid and blood and bits of something that looked like mucus. He returned to Carole and the crying baby. She had found something to tie around the umbilical cord. She showed him where to cut the cord with the scissors. Then, she pulled the child to her and continued to wipe down her body.

The pair looked so natural in the most unnatural environment. Swinging lights overhead cast eerie shadows on the walls as they moved back and forth. The cabinet behind Carole was splintered by stray bullets from the bald man's gun. Yet, in spite of all that, a woman, a man, and a beautiful baby girl sat nestled together in the most perfect and peaceful setting.

"She's all right," she said, looking up and into Allan's eyes.

Her warm, motherly smile twisted into a terrified scream. "Allan!"

Instinctively, he knew the bald man had awakened and was standing behind him. Allan turned and plunged the scissors into the attacker's stomach. The hulking body fell backwards to the floor in shocked pain. Allan crawled on top and pulled the scissors from his gut. Blood began to flow onto the floor around them. Allan raised the scissors above his head, preparing to plunge them into the man's chest, but he couldn't do it. He just needed to push the instrument quickly into his torso and it would all be over, but he could not kill the man. Years of training, of learning, of personal sacrifice, of wanting to help, not hurt, had created an invisible barrier that he could not cross.

The bald man wheezed and moaned on the floor beneath him. His eyes were closed, and his face was covered with great drops of bloody sweat.

Allan searched the man's trousers and found Aunt Julia's cell phone, another phone, and a wallet. He tossed them aside and scrambled to the back wall in search of the pistol. As the big guy began to regain consciousness, Allan's fingers felt the barrel of the gun. He switched to the handle and pointed it in his assailant's direction, purposely aiming high. The bald man's eyes opened wide, and an angry look crossed his face as he focused on Carole standing nearby with the baby. Allan fired.

The sound of the gun seemed to shock the man into consciousness. He quickly glanced at Allan and then scrambled toward the door.

Allan fired again, and the bullet struck the doorframe over his right shoulder. The bald man hit the door and hurdled the stairs on his way outside. He was injured, but Allan and Carole knew he would be back.

Carole knelt beside Allan with Amber clutched to her chest. He dropped his head into her lap and gasped great breaths of lifegiving air. For a brief moment, all was quiet.

In an obscure hotel room late that night, Allan opened the bald man's wallet and examined the contents. His Georgia license identified him as John Sheffield. The wallet contained a couple of credit cards, some American money, and a strange note. It appeared to have been created on a personal printer and cut out to fit the wallet. Allan envisioned the bald man copying it from a website and carefully trimming it with scissors. The title of the note was, "We Watch:"

For those who cannot see for themselves, we watch.

For the helpless, the defenseless, the unborn, we watch.

For those who would protect the helpless, the defenseless, the
unborn, we watch.

For those who oppose liberty, and freedom, and life, we watch.

For the evil, the terrorist, the un-American, we watch.

We watch until the time for watching is over.

LifeWatch

It was a strange verse. Allan figured security professionals might retain such strange poems in their line of work and stuffed it into his own wallet.

They burned Sheffield's wallet to hide the evidence that the man had been there. Allan kept both Aunt Julia's cell phone and the other one the man had carried. He also kept the wristwatch that had fallen from the man's arm during the fight. It was a cheap, unusual analog device, with a heart in the center of the face.

Neither of them could sleep, but Baby Amber slept like, well, a baby. In between feedings and naps, they prepared for the journey ahead.

Carole pulled all of the pertinent data about the Inc.Ubator system together so they could easily recall it whenever they needed to. She stored the files on several storage sites and emailed copies to Allan. Then they saved the files on several thumb drives, just in case.

Allan borrowed scissors and a razor and shaved his head in an effort to hide his identity. He looked hideous. Several heavy scratches from his recent fight lined one side of his scalp, so he had to tenderly maneuver around them with the razor.

"Oh, my God," Carole said when she walked by the bathroom as he toweled himself dry. "You look a lot like Sheffield."

"Thanks, I think," he said. "Do you think it will be enough of a difference to get me by, yet enough to keep my passport legitimate-looking?"

"It might work," she said.

Before the sun rose the next morning, they locked up the apartment, gathered a few important belongings, and set off for the bus station. On the way, they dropped the pistol into the Dane River, beneath the bridge leading to Old Town.

They bought bus tickets to Vilnius, where they intended to catch a flight to Frankfurt and then to America. The five-hour ride would provide them with lots of time to talk and plan their next steps. And to rest.

Watching fields and farmlands pass by the window, Allan asked Carole, "Have I ever told you about my Aunt Julia?"

"Just that Sheffield attacked her and took her phone." They talked quietly so as not to wake Amber.

"She's my favorite aunt," he said, sitting back and letting the hum of the diesel motor settle him. "She's psychic."

Carole gave him the same skeptical look others had given when he described his aunt.

"She lives in Arizona. She used to send me texts and notes to warn me of impending danger. Her warnings actually saved me from the bald man back in Atlanta."

"If you say so," Carole said. "Is she doing okay after the attack?"

"She was hospitalized but should be home by now," he said. "I think we should go see her."

"All the way to Arizona?"

"I think it would be easier for me to get back into the States that way."

"What do you mean?"

"If we fly to Mexico City, we could rent a car, cross the border into Tucson, and then drive up to Phoenix to see her." Carole seemed doubtful. "I'm worried about getting caught by security in Atlanta. If we came in from Mexico and didn't fly to Atlanta, it might be easier."

"I just wish this whole thing were cleared up."

He held her hand. "We'll straighten it all out." He said it wondering how they were going to do that.

By noon, they had boarded a plane in Vilnius bound for Frankfurt.

———————————

Allan picked up a copy of *The New York Times* in a newsstand at the Frankfurt airport. He had been out of country for less than a week, but it felt like half a dozen lifetimes.

They boarded an afternoon flight for Mexico City and paid with Carole's credit card without incident. The new birth certificate and Allan's passport were virtually perfect. While Carole rocked the baby, Allan perused the paper.

The headline "CARLISLE TO RECOMMEND STRONG" leapt out of the front page. He quickly scanned the article, which indicated that Congressman James Carlisle, devastated by his son's death in the recent bombing of the abortion clinic in Atlanta, was planning to announce that he would support Dr. Joseph P. Strong's candidacy for his congressional seat. "Retirement will be a bittersweet pill for us without Dan," he was reported to have said. "It's time for others to take up the fight."

The news came as a real surprise to many in the media. Allan could imagine the news of Dan's death would devastate him, but still, it seemed out of character.

He showed Carole the article and said, "What do you think?"

"Wow. That is a surprise," she said. "Do you think he knew what Dan was really doing?"

"He must have. I don't know why Dan would hide it from him."

"Dan's death must have really overwhelmed him."

"Probably so," he said. But something about the story gnawed at the back of his mind.

FIFTEEN

Mexico City lived up to its low reputation as dusty and grungy. Airport security did little to slow them down. For Allan, traveling as a bald man, with Carole and Amber as his family, seemed to do the trick.

They caught a bumpy flight to Chihuahua, Mexico, later that day. Carole rented a car at the airport, and they headed north toward Phoenix. Allan wished they could have enjoyed the half-day drive as tourists, but they drove like villains, crossing the desert terrain while looking over their shoulders.

The border stop in Agua Prieta was uneventful. They arrived in Phoenix long after dark, exhausted but safe.

Carole checked them into a hotel, and Allan ordered pizza for supper, glad to have good old Italian pizza made the American way, with pepperoni, sausage, and hamburger. It felt good to be back in the USA.

The next morning, after breakfast and a warm, passionate morning shower together, they drove to Aunt Julia's house. Surprise, Arizona, was part of the Phoenix suburbs, in the northwest section of the community.

They approached Aunt Julia's one-story tract house off Paradise Lane and knocked on the door. Mr. Jacoby answered it.

"Hi, Mr. Jacoby," Allan said. "It's me, Allan Chappel."

"Oh, hello, Allan," he said. "I didn't recognize you."

"Well, it has been a while."

"The last time I saw you, you . . ." He held his hand about as high as his hip, palm down. Then he took a closer look. "And you had hair."

"Yeah. What can I say? It's the fad," Allan said, rubbing his palm over his dome. "Is my aunt in?"

"She is. Yes," he said. "Come inside."

They walked back to her room, and Allan knocked lightly on the bedroom door. "Hello? Aunt Julia?"

She was lying in her bed, covered to her chest by a Hopi quilt. "Why, Allan! Come in, come in," she said. "What a wonderful surprise."

"I thought you said she was psychic," Carole whispered in his ear.

"I heard that, young lady," Aunt Julia said. "Don't be snarky with me!"

"Probably the drugs," Allan said softly.

"Usually, drugs make me more tuned in to the psychic forces," she shot back. "This stuff I'm on now gives me the runs."

"I'd like you to meet Dr. Carole Phillips," Allan said, "and Amber Phillips."

"Oh, my goodness," Aunt Julia said. "You are so pretty." She took Carole's hand in her own and clasped it firmly, rubbing the top of it with the fingers of her other hand. "You have a devout soul," she said. And then, to Allan, as if no one else was in the room, "She has a devout soul. She is a good person."

"I know."

Then she turned her attention to Amber. "I knew there was a third."

Carole handed the baby to her. Aunt Julia pulled her close to her chest and kissed her forehead. She ignored the rest of the small crowd in the room for the longest time as she stroked Amber's little bald head and cooed strange noises and rhythmic hymns to her.

Allan looked about the room, pleased to see that his aunt had changed very little. A large, intricate dream catcher hung above the bed. Photographs of his parents, Allan, and Aunt Julia stood in frames on the dresser. Burned-out incense drooped in several different bowls placed around the room. One wall was painted black from top to bottom. The others were orangish-yellow. A large cross hung from a wooden plaque on the wall opposite the dream catcher. Yes, Aunt Julia hadn't changed one bit.

But she did look tired. There were large bruises on her cheeks and arms. A bandage covered a wound on her forehead.

"Mr. Jacoby told me you were mugged," he said. His words interrupted the spiritual bond she was making with Amber.

"How's that? Oh, yes. A big guy, with no hair . . . like you," she said. "What happened to your hair?"

"Just a part of the disguise," he said. "You like it?"

"Hell no," she said. "You always had beautiful hair."

"It'll grow back. Are you doing okay?"

"Every day, in every way, I get better and better."

He didn't know if this was a diagnosis or a pop-psych chant with a bit of sarcasm thrown in.

He reached into his pocket and took out her cell phone. "I found this in Lithuania," he said and placed it gently on the nightstand by her bed.

"She needs more rest," Mr. Jacoby said, pushing through the bedroom door while carrying a tray of coffee cups and a pot of steaming tea. "She won't stay in bed. She has to go to the garden, the kitchen, the mailbox, she does."

"He takes good care of me," she said. "Oh, Darrel. That is so thoughtful of you." The friendly neighbor poured cups for everyone.

"Is this stuff safe?" Carole whispered, and Aunt Julia gave her a glare.

"Probably the safest and best-tasting tea you've ever had," Allan said.

"I don't want to have hallucinations," she said, softer.

Aunt Julia shot her a glance. "I like her, Allan," she said. "She speaks what's on her mind."

"I knew you would," he said. "I'm very lucky."

Carole set aside her partially drunk tea and gently retrieved Amber from Aunt Julia's arms. Reluctantly, the older lady let the baby go.

"So, you're back in the country for now, right?" she said to Allan.

"Yes," he said. "I hope for good."

"It is so wonderful to see you," she said, stretching an aging, sun-marked arm toward him.

He reached out and held her hand.

She didn't move for the longest time. He thought she was dozing off, but then realized she was reading him.

"You're not out of danger yet, my darling angel," she said. "There are many of them, the dangerous ones."

"Why are they after me, Aunt Julia?"

"Because, my child, you threaten them. You imperil their very existence."

"How can I be a threat to anyone?" he asked, desperate.

Aunt Julia said nothing, but silently pointed. All of their eyes followed her finger to Amber.

They headed for Atlanta. The trip was long, and traveling was tough, especially when Amber decided she had had enough, but they made it tolerable by learning more and more about each other.

They stopped for the night somewhere around Abilene, Texas, and while Carole was taking a shower, Allan took out the bald man's cell phone and began to examine it. He made a list of all the recent incoming and outgoing calls. Several names were listed in the phone's contact list, but it only showed first names and phone numbers. Allan recognized Dan's name, the Inc.Ubator offices, and Dr. Chamberlain's office. It made sense that the bald man would have called those numbers since he had been employed by Dan to provide security. Also, Allan figured the bald man would have wanted to keep track of their whereabouts before he killed them. He also found his own name and Aunt Julia's on the contact list. The numbers he didn't recognize, he added to his own list. When he was finished, he had six numbers. He started dialing them to see who might answer.

One was no longer in service.

Two were from Atlanta strip clubs.

He dialed the fourth one, and a friendly voice answered saying, "Thank you for calling LifeWatch. May I help you?"

He apologized and explained that he had dialed the wrong number. After hanging up, he wrote "LifeWatch" on the list.

When he dialed the last two numbers, no one answered, and he was not connected to voicemail. Not much to go on.

The next day, they moved on up the highway and stopped at a Holiday Inn in Ruston, Louisiana, for the second night.

They had breakfast at Denny's in the morning and pressed eastward, finally arriving in Atlanta late at night and checking into a budget motel on the city's west side. They made that their base camp, setting up a place to care for Amber. Carole monitored Amber's progress on her laptop, as the first preemie birthed through the Inc.Ubator process.

After setting up, Carole and Amber lay down for an afternoon nap.

Allan leaned back in the desk chair and watched the two sleeping on the king-sized bed behind him. They looked as peaceful as anyone could possibly be.

Allan longed for more of such peace.

SIXTEEN

After they arrived in Atlanta, Allan wasted no time in his search for answers.

Allan's favorite seminary professor still taught at Emory. Dr. Grady Martin's gifts included the ability to cultivate an intense desire within students to dig deeper and think harder. He had taught several courses on social issues while Allan was in school and had also written a couple of textbooks about social causes. Allan had kept track of some of his work through the years and had even read some of his articles on the pro-life and pro-choice movements. He drove to Emory to look him up and was surprised, but only a bit, that his nameplate hung on the same office door where it was twenty years before.

Looking through the opaque glass window, he could see movement inside. He knocked quietly on the window.

"Yes. Come in," a voice said. Allan opened the door.

Martin was an aging, philosophical sort of guy. He wore an open-collar shirt under a pullover sweater and a tweed jacket, even while in his office. His beard was gray, and he combed over almost every strand of hair he had on top of his head, as if to hide his baldness.

"Dr. Martin?"

"Allan Chappel! My word! Come in. Please, come in."

Allan was a little surprised that the professor recognized him. While Dr. Martin had the memory to remember all of his students, neither Allan's freshly shaven head nor the five-day growth of stubble that had appeared on his chin could hide his identity from his favorite professor. "Have a seat," he said, motioning toward a chair filled with large books about theology.

Allan moved the books off the chair and started to place them on the desk before noticing that the desk was already filled with books and clutter. He finally set them on the floor.

"What have you been up to?" Dr. Martin asked.

It seemed that Dr. Martin had not connected him to the recent reports about the clinic bombing. Allan rubbed his palms together as if to warm them up. "I need your advice. I have an opportunity," he lied, "to join a non-profit organization in the pro-life movement. I know you've researched the movement, and I was hoping you might be able to share your thoughts."

"It would be my pleasure," the elderly professor said, leaning forward on his elbows and tilting his head a little to one side. "The pro-life movement is growing stronger and stronger each year. They have a strategic advantage in their emotional appeal. After all, when you argue that a fetus is alive and abortion is actually taking the life of a living baby, their persuasive argument is difficult to refute."

"So, pro-choice advocates are losing their support?" Allan asked.

"Yes and no," Dr. Martin said. "A solid majority of Americans still support a woman's right to choose. And most political pundits agree that the Supreme Court's decision to overturn Roe awakened a sleeping giant. Apparently, voters didn't like the idea that their right to choose had been taken away, and they made their feelings known during the contentious midterms.

"I see," Allan said.

"Now, if you were looking for a strong ally on the pro-choice side, I'd recommend an attorney named Kimberly Sizemore. She's here in Atlanta and is as sharp as any in her field, especially about reproductive rights." Allan made a mental note.

"Of course," he continued, "if you're really hoping to work with a pro-life firm, you can expect to face Ms. Sizemore eventually. She's passionate about her beliefs."

Dr. Martin leaned back in his desk chair and placed his hands behind his head, elbows out. "Pro-life organizations are alive and well," he said. "And empowered since the recent Supreme Court ruling. And connected. If you're in politics, you want to have this group supporting you."

"What do you mean?"

Dr. Martin stroked his gray beard softly. "The right-to-life lobbies have learned how to inflame their base and rally millions of people to support certain candidates, and, increasingly, to denounce those they disagree with. Again, with a very emotional topic, they have become an extremely powerful lobby group for people who agree with them."

"You said they were connected," Allan said.

"Oh, yes. With political figures and with each other. Some are quite tame, but others are almost as dangerous as some of the neo-Nazi groups in our country. You need to be concerned about the fringe groups. When popular figures inflame their audiences with violent rhetoric, some in the fringe groups become exceedingly dangerous. With the recent Dobbs v. Jackson decision, these fringe groups are even more emboldened. They've had a strong dose of what they've always wanted, and it's made them want more. They're sending death threats to people. They're stalking physicians. They're harassing medical personnel. It seems like they are just a step or two away from taking legal matters into their own hands. They are dangerous.

"Charismatic television and radio personalities who are cavalier with their remarks don't seem to understand the hold they have on these more easily persuadable followers. In my opinion, they are being extremely irresponsible, and their behavior is reprehensible."

"What organizations are we talking about?"

"One I would steer clear of is a group based in Augusta: LifeWatch," he said, looking Allan dead in the eye. "Please tell me you are not working with that group of lunatics."

"Oh, no. Not at all," Allan said and stared back.

"They will kill you, and while in the very act, they will tell you they are fulfilling God's work." Dr. Martin leaned forward on his elbows. "Allan, keep in mind, we are part of a capitalist society. Groups like this rely on money to survive and to grow. Organizations are like live organisms. They protect themselves when threatened. If you threaten to take away their money, you're threatening to take away their power, and those groups are the most volatile."

Allan nodded.

"Just like you or I would run away or fight to protect ourselves if someone threatened us, an organization would do the same thing, on an organizational scale."

Allan studied him closely, wondering why the professor was repeating himself.

Dr. Martin sighed deeply and stood up beside his desk. He held out his hands, palms up. "Allan. I read the papers. I know you are being sought for the bombing of the abortion clinic last week, as well as for murdering several people around the country."

Allan felt the familiar feeling of cold dampness on his palms. He began to imagine escape routes and emergency exits.

"I also don't believe you are one to be capable of committing any of those crimes. Naturally, I could be wrong, but I'm a pretty good judge of character, and a person's character doesn't change that much over time." Allan breathed a little easier.

"From our conversation, I deduct that you believe someone in either the pro-life or pro-choice movements was responsible for the recent deaths. If you can make that connection, you think you can protect yourself." He should have known Dr. Martin would see through him.

"I won't turn you in, Allan, unless they somehow uncover your meeting with me in this office today. Then, I would have to say we talked. But otherwise, I will keep our meeting to myself."

"Thank you, sir."

"The only word of advice I would offer is this," he continued. "Look out for the weaker ones, on the fringe. They are the people who could be most easily manipulated into doing the unthinkable. But it's their leaders who are doing the manipulation." He etched his words in Allan's mind.

Dr. Martin reached across his desk and offered Allan his hand. Allan shook it. "Take care, my friend."

Dr. Martin had told Allan to stay away from LifeWatch, so Allan ignored that advice and attended the LifeWatch rally that night. He drove out to the suburbs, which was filled with McMansions and fine lawns, manicured by people who lived elsewhere. Gated communities and upscale gas stations in shopping centers catering to the well-to-do flashed by his windows.

The campus of Central Church was as big as a small college. Cars filled the expansive parking lot, even on a weekday night. Entire families left SUVs, vans, and exotic autos to file into the cavernous sanctuary for the Save America's Unborn rally. Allan joined the mob and found a seat toward the back and near an exit.

Clearly, LifeWatch was trying to ramp up attendance at tonight's rally. Allan noticed on a program that he received as he entered the rally that LifeWatch had a beefy lineup of speakers scheduled for tonight. The brochure included the announcement that a famous Georgia athlete would be a special guest speaker at this event. Based on the number of vehicles in the parking lot, it worked.

Allan surveyed the folks around him. As far as he could tell, most of them were white, middle-class, and motivated. He didn't see any pregnant women.

He sat through several religious and political songs, a video about the nation's ills, general announcements, the rousing, if disjointed, speech by the Georgia athlete, and a rather lengthy discourse by Joseph Strong, the president and founder of LifeWatch, who followed his talk with an equally lengthy plea for money to keep the organization going. Allan couldn't help but notice that no one mentioned contraception, adoption, or prenatal care for those who can't afford it.

Joseph Strong did mention the need for volunteer support, financial support, and prayer support for LifeWatch. He also suggested that a very few deeply committed, and faithfully obedient individuals consider joining the ranks of the LifeWatch Prime Members by making a special donation. He closed out his presentation by saying, "A very exclusive group of people might become Watchmen, activists who work tirelessly to bring about the goals of the LifeWatch organization. These members proudly wear this wristwatch as evidence of their commitment." He held up his left wrist, revealing his watch. Even from the back of the room, Allan could tell that it was a duplicate of the one he had retrieved from John Sheffield.

At the end of the event, Joseph Strong challenged everyone to complete a commitment card and hand it to the ushers on the way out, with a donation, should they choose to give it. Allan entered his name on the card as "Allan Phillips."

As the crowd filed out of the auditorium, Allan handed his card to one of the ushers. The young man barely looked at the card but stared at Allan's face intently.

"Thank you," he said, "and thank you for coming tonight." He was short and a bit dumpy. His drab tie and wrinkled sports jacket gave the distinct impression that he wasn't wealthy. "And here's some literature that you'll want to read," the usher said, sliding a brochure into Allan's left hand. He brushed his short fingers through his yellow-reddish hair and turned away.

In the parking lot, people gathered in several small groups, talking in low voices. Some seemed angry. Others seemed frightened.

Allan realized that the people about him were drawn into an extremely emotional subject with little more to go on than the words of the men they had just heard. From what he overheard, it didn't seem like they were looking at multiple sides or offering research or background. He wondered how the people from the rally would respond if they knew about Dan Carlisle's ectogenesis system. Would they embrace it or reject it?

Allan climbed into the rental car and pulled on his seatbelt. He tossed the literature on the seat beside him and noticed that it contained more than a brochure. Tucked inside was another card. He pulled the white card out and turned it over. A note was scrawled in pencil on the back.

I know who you are, Allan Chappel. I can help you.
I have information about who destroyed the Inc.Ubator office.
Stay away from Joseph Strong. He's dangerous.
Call my cell phone.
—Keith

He had scribbled his phone number on the bottom of the card.

Sweat peppered the back of Allan's neck as he realized that someone had recognized him. He tucked the card into his shirt pocket and surveyed the parking lot but didn't recognize the usher among the small groups of people scattered here and there.

He cranked the car, hastily exited the parking lot, and headed to the motel with one eye on the mirror to see if someone was following him. He didn't notice anything suspicious.

As Allan recalled the people who had gathered around him at the LifeWatch meeting, caught up in a sweaty fever of emotion, he remembered the mob of antiabortion protestors he had observed near the clinic the day Amanda had died so long ago. Typically, he avoided them, but on that day, he could not contain himself. He'd felt he had to go back to the abortion clinic to face them.

He had driven across town like a man possessed, avoiding other traffic and focusing on the road. He followed the same path he and Amanda had taken to the family clinic.

The mob was there, across the street, smugly waving obscene signs and chanting empty, simplistic slogans. He stopped the car in the middle of the road and climbed out, heading for the guy closest to him. The man could probably tell from Allan's facial expression that he wouldn't join them around a campfire for a marshmallow roast.

"Take it easy, now. We're not doing anything wrong."

"You're doing everything wrong," Allan said and swung his right fist toward the skinny man's jaw. Despite the determined look on Allan's face and his aggressive demeanor, the man never saw the punch coming. He went down like a rag doll.

Another member of the mob rushed over. The man held his sign sideways, like a weapon, to defend himself. "You can't do this."

"You shouldn't be able to do this," Allan said, anger completely consuming him.

"It's our right of free speech," the man yelled.

"Fuck free speech," Allan said and rushed him, pushing him back into the rest of the mob.

"Now hold on there." An older, more confident-looking man spoke up. Pushing his way through the group, he stood before Allan.

"Are you the leader?" Allan asked.

"I'm one of them," he said.

"I have one question for you." Allan panted heavily from his scuffle with the first two protestors and from his intense anger. "How many children have you adopted?"

"What?"

"How many babies have you adopted? You want them to be born. How many have you adopted?"

"I have three wonderful children," he said.

"And how many of them were adopted?" Allan insisted.

"None."

Allan felt his eyes narrowing, as if trying to pierce the man.

"But I didn't make your girlfriend pregnant. It ain't my problem."

"It is your problem. If you're not willing to help ensure the child has a good chance in life, you're not pro-life, you self-serving hypocrite."

The man was stunned but stood his ground. It was obvious that he rarely faced such passionate aggression. Allan turned and walked back to his car.

"You need to meet Jesus," the man yelled after Allan.

"I already have, and he ain't here." He got in his car and drove home.

SEVENTEEN

The next morning, Allan called the number on the back of the card that had been handed to him at the LifeWatch rally, but no one answered. He left his cell number. Then he called Wes.

"Man, are you all right? I thought you'd dropped off the face of the earth."

"That was the plan, wasn't it?"

"Yeah, but...Are you okay?"

"So far," he said. "I'll fill you in over coffee, one day. But for now, I need some help."

"I knew it. You still owe me from last time. I paid forty-six bucks to get my car out of long-term parking at the airport, plus the cab fare to get there."

"I'll repay you."

"Yes, you will."

"Look, Wes. Write this down." Allan gave him a password and one of the web addresses where Carole had stored the Inc.Ubator files. "If anything happens to me, those files will be very valuable. Get ahold of Kimberly Sizemore, of Sizemore & Clark Attorneys. She will help you understand what to do with them."

"Sounds so clandestine," he said.

"I appreciate your help, Wes."

"Paybacks are hellacious," he said.

"Also," Allan began.

"Yesss?"

"If my Aunt Julia calls you, do whatever she asks. She's about all I've got left of my family, so it's important to me."

"Roger, Allan," Wes said, in a lame attempt to be funny.

"There's one more thing," he said.

"What now?"

"Just wanted you to know, I'm a papa."

"What? How can that be?"

"It's a miracle. I've also met a wonderful lady. Her name's Carole."

"I kinda figured that. Congratulations, Bud."

"After all this gets straightened out, we may make it official," he said. "Of course, I'd want you to preach at the wedding." He knew such talk was just guy talk, and that the prospect of a marriage with Carole was, at best, just a possibility. But he did love her and believed that love could grow.

"It'll be my pleasure."

"Thanks, man."

"Is there anything else I can do to help?" Wes asked.

"No. Not yet. But I'll call if there is."

"I know you will," he said.

Sweat soaked the front of Keith's shirt. More sweat dripped down the sides of his chest from his armpits. Keyed up, he drummed his fingers on the steering wheel. He'd been watching the little restaurant that Dr. Strong had entered for over an hour. If he had to wait much longer, he knew he would explode.

The café was a tiny hole-in-the-wall that attracted almost as many Augusta businesspeople as flies. The diner offered nothing but deep-fried, unhealthy food, and comfort-food lovers seemed willing to die for it. Strong ate lunch here at least once a week.

Keith watched through the plate glass window as the two well-suited guests stood up from the table and began their exit. Now was the time. If Keith was going to do this, it was now or never.

He climbed out of his car and walked quickly across the street, heading straight for the café. As he walked through the creaking front door, he almost bumped into Strong's two companions on their exit. He looked toward their table to ensure that Strong was still there. The CEO of LifeWatch was fishing through layers of cash in his wallet.

Keith sat down opposite him. "Have you misplaced some money?" he asked.

Startled, Strong looked up. "What did you say?"

"I was asking if there are funds that you can't account for," Keith answered, almost smugly.

"I was just about to leave a tip," Strong said, pulling a five from his wallet.

"That's not what I'm talking about," Keith answered.

Strong froze. "Perhaps we should have this conversation back at the office."

"No, I feel much safer right here," Keith answered. "I'm never going back to LifeWatch."

Strong stuffed his wallet back into his trousers. "What's this all about?"

Keith leaned forward on his elbows. He actually enjoyed this. He felt a sense of power swell in his chest and realized he might never have another chance to feel this way again. "I have documents that show hundreds of thousands of dollars were slipped out of various LifeWatch accounts and funneled into a private account."

Strong raised his hands in a shrug. "So? We already talked about this."

"Timing is everything," Keith answered. "This all happened just prior to the abortion clinic bombing two weeks ago. I also have obtained documentation that shows the funds were paid to John Sheffield, who used to work in security at LifeWatch."

"This is all preposterous."

"Call it what you want. The documentation doesn't lie."

"Supposing there was some truth to this hoax you've concocted," Strong said, leaning toward his opponent. "What do you plan to do with it?"

"It's not what I plan to do. It's what you will do."

"I don't follow."

"For starters, you'll resign from LifeWatch," Keith said. "You'll contact the police and explain that John Sheffield acted on his own, out of some misguided anger about abortion. Turn him in. I'm sure you can bury the money trail to Sheffield without too much trouble. You've played on people's emotions for personal gain for too long."

"And if I don't?"

"I go to the police. I go to the press. I have what I need to bring you to your knees," Keith said. "You really should be there more often."

"But—"

"Oh, yes. Don't forget, I can always tell the story of Helen the prostitute. About three, four years ago, when I first started with LifeWatch, right?"

"You have no proof about that," Strong said, squeezing his fists so tightly that the knuckles turned white.

"I don't need proof about that. One scandal on top of all the others will just be fuel for the fire."

"Do you want money?"

Keith stood up and pushed the chair back beneath the table. "No, I want justice."

He left the café feeling more nervous than when he went in. He clasped his hands together to prevent them from shaking. He'd done it.

He'd brought down one of the big guys.

EIGHTEEN

The intense pressure from being on the run was wearing on them both. Carole could sense it a mile away. The question was, how to deal with it. Following a quiet breakfast, they chose to visit a nearby park. They had to get outside.

"What else can we do?" Allan asked.

Carole held the baby in a little sling as the couple walked through expansive Piedmont Park. The overcast sky and late fall chill were not enough to chase many people from the hiking and biking trails.

Across the park, a rotund man walking a bulldog introduced his dog to a jogger with a beagle. Instantly, the dogs leapt into aggressive stances and began barking, biting, and growling at each other. It reminded Carole of how people all over the country seemed to be constantly at each other's throats these days—not unlike how she and Allan had been growing tense around each other recently.

"Should I turn myself in?"

"I don't know," she said. She knew he felt like he had no options. "You don't have much of a defense, you know."

"I'm very well aware of that." They walked on in silence.

"We could go to my brother's in Indiana," Carole offered.

"You haven't spoken with him in three years."

"Maybe it's about time to reconnect."

"That's still just running away," Allan said. "We need to find a way to continue to make progress on Dan's process and expose LifeWatch."

"You could call a newspaper reporter," she said.

"I thought they were extinct."

"It might be worth a shot," she said.

"I think we also should go back to the University of Tennessee and see if we can talk Dr. Collins into at least offering us advice and perhaps joining us in a business venture. We can set up another clinic and begin to take steps to legalize the process in the US."

"You also need an attorney," she reminded him.

"You're right." He took her hand. "You know, Dr. Martin mentioned an attorney. He said she was the most authoritative in Atlanta." Allan stared off into the park as if searching for the elusive name. "Sizemore. Kimberly Sizemore. Maybe she can help."

They both seemed visibly calmer now that they were talking and breathing fresh air.

Allan pulled Carole closer and placed his arm around her waist. "Just a little longer," she said.

She almost believed it.

It didn't snow very often in Georgia, and when it did fall, it came down damp and sloppy. When things got wet, it was hell.

Allan watched the woman run out of her office toward her car. He had been standing in the falling snow for over an hour, waiting for her to leave the office to drive back home. Even though he wore a sweater, jacket, and overcoat, he felt iced to the bone.

Kimberly Sizemore, of Sizemore & Clark, had gained respect as one of the South's premier attorneys for gender and reproductive justice. Her discrimination cases had brought her national fame and a healthy fortune. She reached her Jaguar sooner than Allan had anticipated, so he had to half-trot to get close enough to speak with her.

"Ms. Sizemore? Ms. Sizemore, can I speak with you?"

She was trying to extract car keys from a large purse hanging from her arm, and his presence startled her. She looked up with an expression on her face that contained a mixture of fear and embarrassment. "Oh, my," she muttered. Up close, Allan sensed she was older than she looked. Facelifts, Botox, and wrinkle cream had provided a miraculous effect, yet her eyes betrayed her age. Her dark hair was streaked with wisps of stately gray.

"Ms. Sizemore, I just need five minutes of your time."

"Go inside and make an appointment," she said, nodding toward the office complex behind her.

"I may not live that long," he said. "I'll stand outside your car if you will give me a moment to speak with you. I am not armed, and I won't hurt you."

She looked around the lot for help. He assumed she thought the security guard was too far away, so she complied. She opened the driver's door and climbed inside.

For a moment, he thought she might make a run for it, but she rolled down the passenger window halfway. "What can I do for you?"

"My name is Allan," he began. "I need your help." He took a deep breath and exhaled, sending a cloud of breath vapors toward the half-open car window.

He decided on the direct and honest approach. "I am the man the police are searching for regarding Dan Carlisle's clinic."

A look of shock flashed through Ms. Sizemore's eyes. She pressed the starter button on the car, and the engine roared to life.

Before she could put the car into gear, Allan shouted. "I didn't do it!"

That did nothing to stop her. She pulled the stick shift toward her, placing the car in reverse.

"I was there for a job interview!" Allan called.

The Jag began to roll backward.

"It wasn't an abortion clinic!" Allan yelled in desperation.

The car stopped. Ms. Sizemore scrutinized Allan meticulously. "What did you say?"

"Dan Carlisle was not an abortion provider," Allan said, breathing heavily from the cold, stress, and fear. "He had created something better."

She seemed stunned. She hesitated just a moment and then unlocked the car using the switch on her door. "Please sit with me. Let's talk about this."

He opened the passenger door, welcoming the chance to sit on a heated leather seat in the warm interior of her car.

He felt himself beginning to thaw. "I know this sounds unbelievable, but Dan Carlisle had developed a process to extract a living fetus and incubate it until it could survive on its own."

"The subject of ectogenesis has been bandied about for years, but no one is close to making it a reality." She paused and searched his eyes.

"Dan did. One of his associates, Dr. Carole Phillips, and I have a baby back in my hotel room who was birthed using the technique."

"What quantitative proof do you have?" Ms. Sizemore asked.

"All the proof you need," Allan responded with confidence. "We have documentation, photographs, data, everything." He offered the picture on his cell phone of baby Amber in the glass bubble.

She stared at the photo for a long time.

Allan continued, "I'm searching for evidence to prove I'm innocent. When I have it, I'll need an attorney. Would you be willing to help me find someone who would represent me?"

"If I could," Ms. Sizemore said, turning to face him, "I'd represent you myself, but I don't do criminal law. If what you say is true, I won't have any trouble finding the best lawyer in the Southeast to take your case."

"I take it you think people would accept technology like ectogenesis?" Allan asked.

"I think some people would embrace such technology with open arms, as long as they were still given the right to decide for themselves," she said. "If it were forced upon them, I think many would not."

"I need one or two more days; then I will contact you," Allan said, his hand on the door handle.

"Wait," Ms. Sizemore said. "Where is this lab?"

"We had to abandon it in Lithuania. But we have everything we need to duplicate it anywhere in the world. I'll tell you everything in two days," Allan said, opening the door and stepping outside.

She seemed to understand and didn't press him further.

"Thank you, Ms. Sizemore."

"Thank you." She handed him a business card containing her cell number.

Allan returned to his rental car. He steered it out of the parking lot and headed up the street to the ramp that led to I-85 and the hotel. In his rear-view mirror, he watched a large sedan follow his route onto the ramp.

He quickly pulled right and veered off the ramp, just before it was too late. A pickup truck coming up behind him swerved into the middle lane, narrowly missing his bumper.

The sedan swerved off the ramp as well, following three or four car lengths behind.

Allan sped up, passing cars on the left and right, dashing through traffic and narrowly missing a red light. Looking in the mirror, he saw the sedan parked behind other cars at the light. He drove another block and then swerved to the right down a side road. He stayed on that road for a mile, even though he was going away from the motel.

When he was satisfied that he was no longer being followed, he turned around and headed back toward Atlanta.

Allan had never been to Red's Bar in Greensboro, Georgia, before. But when the mysterious man who had given him the note at the LifeWatch meeting finally returned his call, that was the place he chose for them to meet, and it was halfway between Atlanta and Augusta.

"How will I recognize you?" Allan had asked the man. He struggled to remember him from the brief glimpse he'd gotten at the meeting.

"Don't worry. I'll recognize you. Your photo's all over the internet."

After paying the cover, Allan slipped inside, waiting briefly for his eyes to adjust to the dim light. Red's was a small pub with just a handful of customers. Country music blared from a jukebox against one wall.

Allan waited by the door for five minutes, but no one came forward to introduce himself, so he took a seat at the bar and ordered a gin and tonic.

Fifteen minutes and another drink later, a short man in his early thirties took an empty seat beside Allan. "So, how did you like the LifeWatch rally?" he asked.

"I've heard it all before," Allan said.

The man offered his hand to Allan and said, "My name is Keith Edwards. Thanks for meeting me."

Allan shook his hand and replied, "I'll do anything to get to the bottom of this thing."

"Let's go over here, where it's a bit quieter," Keith said.

Allan followed him to a corner table in the back.

"You said you had information that could help me," Allan prompted.

"Let me qualify my information first," Keith said. "I am an accountant for LifeWatch—at least I was until I quit two days ago." He took a long sip of his drink. "God, it's hard for me to believe I actually did it. Of course, my wife won't let me forget it."

Allan nodded.

"Anyway, I stumbled upon some accounts in various departments in that organization, and I noticed that they had been dormant for months. Then, two or three weeks ago, they were all emptied out. I traced the funds and found that they were all deposited into the same private account." He handed Allan several photocopies showing various columns of numbers and bank accounts.

"I'm not an accountant," Allan interrupted. "Is this kind of thing uncommon?"

"For LifeWatch it is," he said. "I also did a little clandestine research and found that a man named John Sheffield had withdrawn all of the money from the private account. Turns out that Sheffield used to work in security at LifeWatch."

Allan felt a chill run through him. He pulled out the driver's license that he had taken from Sheffield's wallet and showed it to Keith. "Is this the guy?"

Keith nodded. "That's him."

Allan frowned deeply and said, "But that's not really much to go on. After all, maybe he's just doing some consulting work that affects several different departments."

"Well, let me tell you," Keith said. "I confronted Dr. Joseph Strong about this yesterday, and he couldn't deny it."

"That's not enough to take to the police," Allan persisted. "Why would Strong hire Sheffield to stop Dan Carlisle?"

"I don't know anything about Carlisle's business, but it must have threatened Dr. Strong. He always claimed to hate abortions, but I know personally that he didn't give a shit either way. Still, he would never go that far to stop another abortion clinic."

Allan wondered what Keith knew but was not saying. He said, "Yeah, but Dan wasn't running an abortion clinic ... How much does LifeWatch bring in each year?"

"Over twenty million dollars."

Allan snapped his fingers. "Strong wouldn't care if Dan performed abortions. But if Strong believed Carlisle's process would render abortions unnecessary, Strong's entire mission would shut down. That would threaten him. Strong has used the pro-life movement for years to make a fortune. Without abortions, he would have nothing."

"You may have nothing to worry about," Keith said. "I told Strong I wouldn't tell the press or police about this if he turned Sheffield in. If he does, then that will clear any involvement on your part."

Allan thought long and hard. It just didn't seem like enough to go on. He folded Keith's accounting notes and stuffed them in his jacket pocket. "I appreciate the information. Would you be willing to tell that to a police inspector?"

"Let's give Strong another day to turn Sheffield in, and if he doesn't do anything, I'll call."

Allan gave him Inspector Johnson's card. "Here's the guy."

"I don't think you need to worry at all," Keith said. "He looked so scared when I told him that I had documentation, I think he may have wet himself."

Allan felt better about this news than any he had received in a long, long time.

Keith walked with him to the front door. Allan pulled out his keys and was headed toward his parked rental when he heard the squeal of wheels against asphalt and saw a white SUV careen around the corner. With instincts frayed over the last two weeks, he instantly jumped back from the curb and pressed himself against the concrete block wall of the building behind him.

The vehicle sped past him, but seconds later smashed into a young man walking across the street. Screams and yells echoed through the streets and alleys. Allan recognized Keith's body as it was thrown down the street and into the side of panel truck. As quickly as it had come, the SUV drove off into the night.

Allan ran to the site of the accident and found a small crowd of men gathered around the crumpled body of Keith Edwards. Someone called 911, and he heard sirens in the distance. Allan turned and headed back to his rental, climbed inside, and drove off.

Keith was dead, but the driver had missed Allan. Once again, luck was on his side. He knew it wouldn't last forever.

NINETEEN

"Oh, my God," Carole exclaimed, hands covering her mouth as she struggled to breathe. "We have to get out of here. It's just a matter of time until they find us." Allan's report on the meeting with Keith Edwards had scared the hell out of her.

"Keith gave me his notes," he said, holding the folded copies Keith had given him in the bar. "Joseph Strong is slime. I want to see his face when I show him this."

"No," Carole cried. "We have to leave. They will kill you."

Allan was not going to back down. "I'm going to LifeWatch tomorrow."

"If you leave us tomorrow, we will never see you alive again."

"I have to try."

Carole stared at him for an interminable minute. The fear in her eyes softened, but just a bit. "You might not be able to get close to him," she said. "I'll go."

Late in the afternoon, they walked up the steps to the front doors of the LifeWatch headquarters as a family. Allan had Amber strapped to his chest in a baby sling. They joined the four o'clock tour group in the lobby and followed the vivacious tour guide up the elevator to the fourteenth floor. The tour wound through the accounting department with people in cubicles, eyes glued to their computer screens, past video editing bays where LifeWatch commercials ran nonstop on overhead monitors, and down corridors flanked by offices before stopping at an open set of double doors. "This is Dr. Joseph Strong's office," the tour guide announced. Strong sat at his massive desk, talking on the phone. He looked up, grinned a million-dollar smile, and waved at the tour group passing by his door.

Carole slipped to the back when the group stopped in the doorway of a large room filled with employees talking into telephone headsets. "These agents take calls about the mission of the organization and provide pregnancy counseling," the guide whispered. "They attend rigorous training before donning those headsets."

Even from the hallway, Carole could sense the sincerity the LifeWatch call center agents showed as they earnestly talked with distressed people over their headsets. If only the LifeWatch organization would embrace the Carlisle ectogenesis process, things could be so different!

At the front of the group, Allan raised his hand. "Do they give advice on contraception?"

"Oh, no. Most of the people who call are well past the point at which contraception might help," the guide said.

"What about adoption?" Allan asked.

The tour guide looked slightly irritated. "I believe we refer callers to a list of national adoption agencies on our website. However, our main goal is to try to keep children in the family with their biological father and mother ... as God intended."

Everyone in the group was focused on the tour guide and Allan as Carole began to back down the hall toward Joseph Strong's office. She hated how he was obviously using the employees in his organization for financial gain and personal power. She slipped through the open double doors, turned around, and closed them gently behind her. When the lock on the door clicked, Strong looked up from his desk.

"I believe the tour group is down the hall," he offered.

"I don't care about the tour group," Carole said, striding toward the seated executive.

"I beg your pardon?"

"I want to talk about Dan Carlisle."

As if he had rehearsed, Strong shook his head slowly. "Such a sad loss," he said. "I don't know how he could have involved himself in such an evil practice."

"Unless, of course, the abortion story was just a cover-up of some sort," Carole said.

"I don't think I follow you," Strong said.

"I knew Dan Carlisle, and he was not an abortion provider," she challenged. "Not that there would be anything wrong with that."

Strong did nothing to hide his shock. "I really don't know anything about that."

"I think you might."

"Let me call the tour desk," Strong said, picking up the phone.

"The problem is, Dr. Strong, when you use violent and emotional rhetoric like you do, you inflame a lot of people."

"I think it's time for you to leave." Strong stood up.

"Some people, the emotionally weak and easily persuadable ones, may take your words literally. When you say someone needs to stop what they're doing, these people believe they are responsible for making these individuals stop."

"This is preposterous," he said and started to make his way to his desk.

Carole stepped in front of him. "James von Brunn was such a person. He killed a security guard in the Holocaust Museum."

"You need to leave, now."

"Shelley Shannon shot Dr. George Tiller because he performed abortions."

"I had nothing to do with that."

"Several years later, Scott Roeder shot Dr. Tiller through the eye and killed him in his own church."

"Maybe the man deserved to die."

"In America, no one deserves to die without a trial. Tiller did not commit a crime."

"He committed the crime of murder in the eyes of God!"

"Then let God convict him," Carole said. "It's that kind of talk that causes the weak to do the unspeakable, and you don't care!"

"I care about the half a million babies who will be murdered in our country this year."

"Your careless rants have caused people like von Brunn, Shannon, and Roeder to do terrible, unjust deeds. People die because of the irresponsible rhetoric people like you spew out around our country."

"This is ridiculous," Strong said, glaring at her, trying to stare her down.

"Like John Sheffield."

Strong's eyes narrowed down to laser points.

"Yes. John Sheffield was an employee of yours, wasn't he?"

"Our organization is blessed to have many people who work for our cause. Unfortunately, it's impossible for me to know everyone."

"Oh, you'd recognize him. He had one of your special watches," Carole said, tossing Sheffield's watch on the desk.

"We've given away over a hundred of those through the years." Tiny drops of perspiration were forming on Strong's forehead.

"Sheffield was one of your special ones, wasn't he?" Strong said nothing. "He was a Watchman. He infiltrated Dan Carlisle's office, and when you realized his medical techniques would end your lock on power and your lucrative revenue stream, you had Sheffield destroy it." Strong pressed some keys on his phone.

Reaching into her jacket, Carole pulled out copies of the accounting logs Keith Edwards had given Allan and tossed them on Strong's desk. "I have proof. Keith Edwards gave us these last night before you had him killed."

"I had nothing to do with that, either."

"Then Sheffield did it, and you manipulated Sheffield for years."

"Tom! Get someone up here immediately," Strong shouted into the phone.

Carole wasted no time. She sprinted from the office and down the hall to a door beneath an exit sign. Taking the steps two at a time, she ran, breathless, through a back door into the parking lot.

Allan was waiting in the rental car. Amber was already buckled into her child's seat. Carole dove into the passenger seat, and he sped off through the parking lot, down the road toward the highway and Atlanta.

Adrenaline flooded Allan's brain. He sped up the car and constantly searched the mirror. He steered the car west on Interstate 20, toward Atlanta and Inspector Johnson's office.

An SUV pulled up behind them.

He drove on, waiting for it to pass on the left and speed off into the darkness.

It came closer.

Allan sped up a bit.

The SUV came even closer, almost on their bumper.

He felt his palms become moist on the steering wheel. He gripped it tighter and pulled the car into the left lane.

The vehicle behind him followed.

He stepped on the gas and sped ahead, but the other vehicle caught up. He squinted in the rearview mirror to make out the model. The driver turned on his bright lights.

He sped up more, unable to shake the tailgater.

Allan pressed on the brakes, and the car started to slow. The SUV mimicked their actions, at first. But then, as if the driver could tell what Allan was doing, it edged up closer again.

The SUV's bumper banged into theirs. Allan saw Carole snap back into her seat out of the corner of his eye. The SUV bumped them again. This time, she was ready and was sitting with her head back against the headrest.

The faster he drove, the faster the SUV pursued. He swerved from one lane to another but couldn't shake the vehicle.

He swerved left again just as the SUV accelerated and caught their left fender behind the tire. The rental car went into a tailspin, out of control and sliding down the interstate highway. Car headlights zoomed by the windshield, leaving spinning trails. After one final, firm bump, they flipped sideways, rolling three times before coming to a stop in the median.

The car was disturbingly silent, with only a creak and a moan here and there. Allan unbuckled his seatbelt and climbed out of the car. A crowd was gathering.

"You'd better be still there, sonny," someone said.

"Ambulance is on its way."

Allan looked down the highway and saw the SUV parked on the other side of the road, its occupant watching from a distance, his eyes piercing, fixed on him across the dark stretch of lanes. Dizzy, dazed, and stunned, he felt like he was watching everything from somewhere outside of himself, detached from the reality around him.

Red and yellow lights announced the coming of the ambulance and fire trucks. Carole was strapped onto a flat board and carried off to the ambulance. When Allan caught sight of the baby-sized board on which Amber was strapped, his heart sank. A team of EMTs gathered around her, working feverishly. Allan denied a gurney and climbed into the back with Carole and Amber.

The ride to Grady Hospital took less than twenty minutes. Allan tried to answer the EMT's questions as well as he could in the fog that surrounded him.

The three of them were taken to the emergency room for treatment. Allan found it hard not to hold and cuddle Amber while she cried in fear.

Eventually, they sedated her and put an IV into her tiny arm. Carole was also sedated, and finally the two were admitted to rooms in the hospital.

Allan explained to the people in the emergency room that they did not have insurance. They were US citizens, he said, but had just moved to the States from Lithuania. He was given several forms to complete.

When two police officers entered the emergency room, Allan ducked down the hall to avoid them. He didn't want to answer questions that might reveal his identity. Eventually, he found his way to Carole's room.

She was sleeping soundly, her neck in a thick brace.

A doctor found him in her room.

"Mr. Phillips," he said.

Allan had heard somewhere that if they called you by your first name, then the news might be bad. If they called you by your last name, the news was bad.

"I'm afraid your baby didn't make it. I'm so sorry."

Tears began to flow. "She was very young, wasn't she?"

Allan nodded.

"An accident like this one is tough on infants. She had internal injuries, and we just couldn't prevent it."

He wiped his nose with his sleeve, not caring how it looked or sounded. The doctor said, "Your wife is going to need a lot of support."

"Okay," Allan muttered.

"You're going to need some rest, too," the doctor added. "There's a motel across the street that helps people in your situation. Would you like me to ask one of the aides to set it up for you?" He nodded.

"Take care of yourself, Mr. Phillips," he said. "You'll get through this."

Allan had often wondered who designed chapels for hospitals and airports. Those tiny refuges of hope and despair, hardly larger than a big closet, were always so nondescript, generic, and politically correct. He had imagined it would take an unusual someone to design something so completely respectful.

At the moment, however, he couldn't care less. He was just grateful for a place he could be alone.

He knelt on the floor before the altar table and cried as he had not cried in twenty years. He cried for his daughter, snatched from a pre-birth death, only to be killed by the very people who claimed they were trying to prevent such deaths.

He thought about how Amber would not be able to enjoy a life in this wonderful country, away from the hardships of a life of poverty on the streets of a young European nation. He thought about how she would not have a first day in elementary school, or a first date, or a prom, or college, or a wedding. He cried for her as only a father might cry for his deceased daughter.

When he was done, he was so exhausted he felt he couldn't get up. The stress and pressure of the last two weeks, the pain of losing a loved one and almost losing another, and the anxiety and tension combined to make him feel as weak and helpless as he had ever felt.

He was ready to give up, to give in.

Then his cell phone buzzed. Aunt Julia's text said, *Call Wes.*

Exhausted, defeated, and irritated at one more thing to do, he started to tuck the phone into his pocket but caught himself. Recalling previous problems caused by ignoring Aunt Julia's warnings, he pushed the speed dial button for Wes's phone and leaned back against the wooden table in the tiny chapel.

"What's up?" Wes answered.

Just then, light flashed into the dark chapel from the hallway as the door opened.

"Hello, Allan," a gruff and frighteningly familiar voice said.

John Sheffield's shadow ominously filled the doorway. He walked menacingly inside the chapel and let the door close behind him.

"John Sheffield," Allan hissed. He laid the cell phone down on the floor. "How did you find me?"

"Allan. I used the GPS on your phone to find you in Europe. I did the same thing with the GPS on the phone you took from me. We learned a lot about tracking technology in the Marines."

How could I have been so stupid, Allan thought, shaking his head. "You were a Marine, right? Where did you serve?"

"I *am* a Marine," John shot back. "'Once a Marine, Always a Marine.' I served two tours in Afghanistan, and I've been following you since you returned to America."

"What do you want?"

"I will kill you." He walked the few steps to the front of the chapel.

"Why?"

"Because of all that you stand for. Because you kill innocent babies. Because you are evil."

"Who told you that?"

"Everyone at LifeWatch. Dr. Strong."

"Did Dr. Strong also tell you the Atlanta office was an abortion clinic?"

"He called it an abortion research facility and said they were coming up with new ways to kill babies."

"That's not true."

"That's what you were doing when I found you in Lithuania," Sheffield snapped.

"We weren't aborting a baby, John. We incubated it so it would live and not be aborted."

A distinct look of disbelief crossed the big guy's face. He blinked several times. "That's not possible."

"It is."

"I don't believe you."

"In fact," Allan added, "the baby we brought to the States was that child. We raised it from a fetus to its present state."

John shook his head, as if to shake away the confusion and pain. "It! It! The baby is not an it!"

"You're right, John," Allan said, trying to calm the big man down. "Her name was Amber, and we adopted her as our own. She would have been aborted, but we, that is Dr. Phillips and Dr. Carlisle, found a way to keep her alive until she could survive on her own."

"That's not possible."

"Not only possible," Allan said, "it really happened."

John was shaking his head back and forth. "Stop! You're trying to trick me," he said, sweat dripping from his nose.

"I don't know what to tell you, John. The baby that died tonight was the one you saw with Dr. Phillips in Klaipeda."

"The baby died?"

Allan choked back a tear. It was too soon to talk about this calmly. He breathed in deeply. "Yes. When our car flipped over, her fragile body couldn't take the impact. Baby Amber died just a few minutes ago."

John seemed paralyzed in thought. Seconds ticked slowly by. He stared intently at the generic stained-glass window at the front of the chapel.

Allan did not move.

"John," Allan said. "You said you're a Marine. You've lost some of your brothers, right?"

Sheffield nodded.

"You suffered over there, right?"

Sheffield said nothing but kept staring at the stained-glass window.

"John," Allan said, lowering his voice. "People took advantage of you. People used you."

The big guy shook his head slowly and turned his eyes toward the ground. "Dr. Strong used you."

John was silent.

"Why—" he said, almost whispering.

"What?"

"Why—?"

Allan tried to keep his answer simple and straightforward. "She was young, John. She was born prematurely."

"No," he answered. "That's not what I'm asking." He looked up and into Allan's face. "In Lithuania, why didn't you kill me when you had the chance?" he asked.

"I couldn't, John," Allan said. "I thought that I should have—we needed to kill you to stay safe—but I couldn't do it."

John dwelt longer on that. "And you are working to save little babies?" he said. His forehead furrowed with worry. "But why would Dr. Strong tell me you were experimenting on babies before they were born? Why would he lie?"

Allan could have tried to explain that Strong was taking advantage of the opportunity to break into the political field. He could have told him that people paid Strong because they thought he was committed to stopping abortions. He could have tried to describe Strong as he actually was: an opportunist who wouldn't let anyone, living or dead, get in his way. But none of those reasons would have made a difference.

"I don't think I know that, John," Allan said.

John stuffed the pistol in his jacket pocket, which made Allan feel much safer. "So, what do you do now?" John said, almost monotone.

"We have to find a way to prove that Dr. Strong was behind Dan Carlisle's death, and the deaths of the others who worked with him."

"I thought Carlisle was killing babies," John said.

"I know. But now you know you were fooled."

"Yeah."

"John," Allan said, leaning closer, "you can help us. You can set this thing straight for us. Would you be willing to testify that Dr. Strong set you up for the killings and the office bombing?"

He looked up from the floor. "Really? No, I couldn't do that. I don't talk in public."

"John, if you help us, we can help thousands of children through this process. Would you talk with the police?"

He shook his head again.

"We need to go there," Allan added. "We'll go talk with Inspector Johnson. What would you tell him, if you could?" Allan asked.

John looked up and said, "I'd tell them that Dr. Strong confused me and said I was saving babies, so I killed Dr. Carlisle and the others. Dr. Strong said I would save little babies."

"That wouldn't be so hard to say to the police, would it, John?"

"I can't!" he shouted. A determined look crossed his face. "But I can stop Dr. Strong." He turned and marched toward the chapel door.

"No, wait, John," Allan called. "Go with me to the inspector's office."

"You go there," John said. "I have to go someplace else." The door flew open, and John walked through it. In moments, he was gone, and Allan was alone in the chapel. Picking up his cell phone, he noticed that the call was still connected.

He hung up and stuffed the phone into his pocket.

He needed rest.

TWENTY

Allan slept for five hours and awoke in a sweat.

Strong's press conference was today, and Allan was convinced Sheffield would attempt to kill Strong at the press conference.

He quickly dressed and headed down to grab breakfast at the diner across the street from the motel. He thought about the scene that would surely unfold later that day. He felt odd. He should have been glad that the man who had killed his daughter and the Inc.Ubator employees was about to kill the man who had started this mess, but he didn't. Inside, a powerful sense of justice and compassion won over his feelings of anger and hate. He knew that no matter what Joseph Strong had done, it wasn't right that he should die. Not this way, if at all.

As he watched from the diner window, two police cars pulled into the motel parking lot. Inspector Johnson sprung out of one of the cars and dashed into the lobby. A few minutes later, he came out with a motel employee. He unlocked Allan's room and, guns drawn, ran inside, only to find it empty.

Allan thought long and hard about telling Johnson about Sheffield. He could stop Sheffield at the rally, and he could arrest Strong if he believed Allan's story. But he probably wouldn't, and there was no way for Allan to convince him. How could he describe the seemingly impossible to an unbeliever?

He paid for his breakfast and exited the diner in the opposite direction, away from the motel. He called a cab and took it south on I-75. Slumped in the backseat, he phoned Wesley.

"You are hot," Wes said. "I've had police hounding me for days. You need to turn yourself in."

"I will, as soon as I'm ready."

"Listen, man. It's over. I heard the bald man's confession through your cell phone," Wes said. "I recorded the whole thing and sent it to Inspector Johnson. We have the proof we need."

"If that's true, why did Inspector Johnson raid my hotel room this morning?"

"Probably for your own protection," he said. "You need to come in now before someone gets hurt."

"Look, Wes. I've got to stop Sheffield. Can I borrow your car?" Allan asked.

"I'd loan it to you, but it's in the shop over on Pryor and Thornton." It was odd for Wes to specify the location of an auto repair shop.

"Damn! I was hoping to use it."

"Sorry, man. The mechanic said it would take a couple of days to fix the transmission. I'm heading over to Pryor and Thornton now to check on it."

Allan sensed Wes was sending a coded message. "Look, Wes," Allan said. "As soon as I've gotten this mess straightened out, I'll turn myself in to Inspector Johnson. I need a little more time."

"Be careful, Allan," Wes said.

―――――――――――

There was no auto repair shop on the corner of Pryor and Thornton. However, there was a YMCA, and in the parking lot sat Wes's Volvo.

Allan had the cab driver drive by the parking lot and circle back around to drop him off about two blocks away. He hiked over to the Y's parking lot.

He waited in the shadows for over an hour and saw no sign of police. He guessed they hadn't followed Wes's hints.

He tried the car doors, but Wes had locked them. "Come on, man," Allan said out loud. "How am I supposed to get in?"

He looked through the passenger window and couldn't see the keys anywhere. When he pulled back from the car, he noticed his breath had fogged the window. "Come inside" was written on the foggy window surface.

He turned around and strolled over to the YMCA, like any other member. An employee was at the sign-in desk, but he told her he was meeting a friend. She let him go inside.

He found Wes in the weight room, sweating like a criminal on death row. "Allan!" he said. "What took you so long? I've been here for two hours."

"Sorry," he said. "It took longer than I thought it would."

"I don't want to know." He tossed Allan his car keys.

"I've got real bad news," Allan said.

Wes came closer and rubbed a towel through his hair.

"Carole's in the hospital. We had an accident."

"Man, I'm sorry."

"We lost the baby."

"I can't imagine ..." Wes said, grabbing him and giving him a warm hug.

Allan pulled away and said, "Gotta go."

Wes threw a black hooded sweatshirt to him. "You might need this," he said.

"You are a lifesaver." Allan pulled the sweatshirt over his head. "One more thing."

"What now?"

"Do you own a gun?"

The Old Medical College building had housed the Medical College of Georgia from 1835 until 1911. Six gigantic columns graced the portico, giving it a distinctive, congressional feel. On this day, the steps were filled with reporters of all stripes. Traditional newspaper reporters mingled with those from television and radio to get the official word on Congressman Carlisle's endorsement. There were even a few web bloggers armed with smart phones and tablets. In addition, hundreds of supporters carried pro-life signs and chanted pro-life slogans in support of Dr. Joseph Strong.

Allan stayed in the back of the group, his hands in his pockets and his head covered by the hooded sweatshirt that Wes had loaned him. He didn't know what he was going to do. He only hoped that he could find Sheffield before he attempted to kill Strong. Then, he could reveal Dr. Strong and his LifeWatch group for what they really were.

Several times, on the drive from the YMCA to Augusta, he had tried to talk himself out of what he was about to do. Most men would consider it ironic fate if Sheffield were to kill Strong. Many might even wish it.

But Allan couldn't do that. Just as he couldn't find it within himself to kill Sheffield in the struggle at the laboratory in Klaipeda, he couldn't allow the big guy to take justice into his own hands once again. If justice were to be dealt, there was a system to do that.

The press conference was supposed to start at one o'clock, but no one was surprised when the time slipped by. Then, at 1:20, Congressman Carlisle, Dr. Strong, and several other men in suits came out of the front doors and approached the microphones. Three bodyguards escorted them onto the stage. At first, he thought one of them was John Sheffield, but upon closer scrutiny, he realized that Sheffield wasn't among them. They stood with their arms across their chests behind Carlisle, Strong, and the other suits. The crowd erupted into thunderous applause. The congressman held up a hand to quiet the crowd, and Dr. Strong stood beside him, grinning like a jack-o'-lantern.

"I want to thank you all for coming out to our press conference today," the congressman began.

Allan searched the crowd for the familiar face of John Sheffield. To his relief and fear, he didn't see him.

"A few days ago," Carlisle continued, "I told you that I would not be campaigning for my seat in Congress. That was one of the most difficult speeches I have ever given." His face seemed pale, and his voice lacked his usual Southern-effeminate flair. He seemed to be focused on just getting through the speech. He continued, "Today, this speech will be one of the easiest. I'm here with good news. I'm here to publicly endorse the one man whom I truly believe will keep up the good fight I have fought." The crowd applauded again.

"I am here to introduce a man of integrity and honor, a God-fearing man who will help put our country back on the right track." Allan continued his vigilant search of the crowd.

A strong hand closed around his left arm. He quickly turned to the weathered face of Inspector Johnson. "Let's not interrupt the good congressman just yet, son," he said.

It was over. Allan felt the strength drain from his shoulders.

"Don't look so down, my friend," the inspector said. "You know what they say about the fat lady? I don't think she's even stepped up to the stage yet."

"How'd you find me?" he asked.

"We got a phone call from your look-alike, Reverend Wes Blake."

Johnson pushed him through the crowd, his hand on his arm like a vise. They moved to the side, away from the cameras, reporters, and supporters. "We know what he's gonna say, now, don't we? Let's skip this little presentation."

"But you don't understand. John Sheffield will be here today. He's going to try to kill Joseph Strong."

Just then, the doors opened behind the podium. A fourth person slipped through the door and stood in the back behind the other bodyguards. No one seemed to notice him, except Allan.

"That's him. Sheffield. He's going to kill Strong." Allan wrestled free from the inspector's tight grasp just as John Sheffield slid a beefy hand into his sport jacket.

Carlisle upped the tempo and said, "The fight will continue because our cause is a just cause. The man who will lead us to victory is a just man. He is with me on this stage, today. Please welcome my friend and colleague, Dr. Joseph P. Strong!"

Strong was striding toward the podium when Sheffield drew a .38 caliber pistol and took aim.

Allan took the steps three at a time. "John. No!"

The other three bodyguards saw Allan approaching and immediately went into action, charging toward him. Two drew their own pistols and aimed them at him.

Sheffield hesitated for a second and turned toward Allan.

The closest guard fired his pistol into Allan's stomach, stopping the crusader cold. The other two guards grabbed him and wrestled him to the floor. The crowd screamed.

Carlisle and Strong backed away from the brawl in shock.

Sheffield, seeing Allan was stopped, turned and aimed his pistol at Strong.

Two more shots exploded, and the crowd screamed in horror. Strong clutched his chest and backed away from Sheffield.

But Sheffield's gun remained silent. Two holes in his massive chest began to ooze dark-colored blood. He stumbled back a step and collapsed to the deck just as Inspector Johnson, gun drawn, charged the stage. He turned his attention to the three bodyguards who had tackled Allan. "Get off him!" he yelled. Then, to everyone else on the stage, above the chaos of the crowd, he shouted, "Stay right where you are! I'm Inspector Nelson Johnson with the Atlanta Police Department." He pointed the gun from one person to the next until they all became still.

Allan felt tired. He wanted to stop running. He only wanted to rest.

TWENTY-ONE

Some doctor was shining a bright light in his eyes. He squinted and tried to turn his head away. The movement made his chest hurt.

"Allan Chappel?"

"Yes."

"Do you know where you are?"

"No. Should I?"

"Do you know what day it is?"

"I have no idea."

"He's fine."

Allan looked around the hospital room. A TV hung from the ceiling in front of his bed. A beige wardrobe was against one wall and a porcelain sink stood next to it. There were a couple of guest chairs on one side of the room. Fluorescent lights hung from the ceiling. A couple of doors were against another wall. He assumed one led to a bathroom and the other, which held a thin pane of glass, to the hallway outside.

Wes was standing beside his bed.

"Don't you have anything better to do?" Allan asked his favorite minister.

"Just lookin' after my parish," Wes replied.

The doctor added, "He's been here every day to see you."

"How long have I been out?"

"This would be day four," Wes said.

Allan focused on Wes. He looked tired. Allan admired his commitment. "Thanks, man."

Inspector Johnson came over to take the doctor's place beside his bed. "You were shot, son," he said.

"No shit. They made you an inspector for being able to figure out stuff like that?"

He chuckled and then turned serious. "John Sheffield died at the scene."

The news disturbed Allan, although, on the surface, he thought it shouldn't. In a sense, he felt that he had failed to keep Sheffield from hurting himself or others.

"You're an exceptionally lucky man."

"Yeah," Allan said. "I've heard you say that before."

"We've also detained Dr. Joseph P. Strong for conspiracy to commit murder on several counts. The national news networks announced that the LifeWatch board of directors is meeting to figure out what to do next."

"No more life for LifeWatch, right?" Allan wondered what medications he had taken. "You have been busy, Inspector," he said.

"This is going to take a while to sort out. Good thing you already have an attorney."

Just then, as if on cue, the door to the hallway opened, and Kimberly Sizemore stepped inside, talking to someone through a headset. "I'll need confirmation on that by noon." She clicked off the device and then turned to the men in the room. "I told you to call me the minute he woke up," she said.

"Speak of the devil," Johnson said. "Ms. Sizemore," he added, "we did. It just took you a while to get to the hospital."

"You know you aren't supposed to question the witness without his counsel being present," she snapped.

"Tell me, Allan. Did I question you?" Inspector Johnson asked.

"Ruthlessly," he said.

"So what did you say?" Ms. Sizemore asked.

"He told me that Joseph Strong has been arrested and that I need a lawyer. Can you recommend any?"

"That's it?" Ms. Sizemore asked.

The inspector said, "That's about it."

Wes raised his right hand. "Scout's honor."

"But what I want to know the most—" Allan said to Wes. "How is Carole? Is she okay?"

Wes stepped closer and said, "She was released yesterday. She was pretty banged up, but she's healing nicely. We've arranged a short-term apartment for her not far from here."

"Thanks, my friend."

"How's she taking the news about Amber?"

"Pretty hard," Wes said. "We've connected her with a grief counselor."

"How much longer do I have to stay here?"

"A couple of days and we'll see how it goes," the doctor said.

"I'll bring Carole by later this afternoon," Wes said. Then he added, "Let me tell you, you made a smart choice in her. She's a strong and confident lady."

Allan knew Wes was right. However, he would also add "restless" to the description, and that concerned him.

True to his always-truthful word, Wes softly entered the room late in the day and held the door open for Carole.

She looked rough. Bruises marked her cheeks and hands. Her eyes were puffy.

But she looked wonderful to Allan.

She rushed over to the bed and hugged and kissed him gently.

"I'll be outside, if you need me," Wes said, but neither of them seemed to hear him.

"I missed you," Allan said.

"How could you? I heard you've been asleep for several days."

"I missed you in my dreams," he said.

"That sounds so sad."

"It was."

They kissed again.

Carole pulled back and tears filled her eyes. "We lost our baby," she cried.

"I know," he said and pulled her close.

They both cried hard and long.

He thought again of the little girl in the glass ball whom he had watched move and grow just a few days before.

"We've gotta let her go," Allan said.

"I don't know if I can. It's not easy."

"It's not supposed to be easy."

Winter weather had settled in early. Forty or fifty people—friends, family, and members of Wesley's church—huddled in the drafty sanctuary for Amber's funeral service. The Asbury Singers performed several of the most stirring spirituals Allan had ever heard. One soloist, the woman Wes had said could really belt out the blues, sang "Jesus Loves the Little Children" a cappella, and Allan didn't think he would ever forget it.

Wes did a magnificent job saying the eulogy. "Little Amber was very normal, but also very special. She was born in a new way, and in so doing, opened the door for many more like her. And tragically, she was the first baby birthed by this new method to die." Carole gripped Allan's hand tighter.

He described how much she had been loved by Carole and Allan in the few days of her life. And he closed by saying Little Amber had been lost, but then saved, only to be lost again. He prayed she would find eternal safety in the loving arms of God.

The gravesite service was altogether different. The forty or fifty who had come together at Asbury United Methodist Church were joined by over two hundred news and television reporters and crew, with microphones extended and cameras rolling.

For Carole and Allan, the cold wind seemed even colder by the gravesite as the tiny casket was lowered into the ground. The presence of so many whom they didn't know and who really didn't care made it all the more difficult.

On the way back to the limousine, the questions the reporters asked became more and more insensitive.

"Do you know who the real parents were?"

"Since Amber was born unusually, did she act unusually?"

"Did she have any quirks or strange behaviors?"

"Do you think this was God's way of telling you the process was wrong?"

They had chosen rude names for Amber. One network named her "Ambitious Amber." Another falsely referred to her as a "test tube baby." A third outdid them all by calling her the "Bubble Baby."

Allan wrapped his arms around Carole and held her tightly to deflect the callous questions being asked for personal profit. They were both weak and wounded, and the questions did nothing but hurt them more.

But somehow, he had to believe that the little girl he had first met in a glass globe had started a new way of living and caring for those about them. He had to believe it because it was true.

A couple of days later, Carole and Allan met with Kimberly Sizemore in her office in Buckhead. Kimberly had personally called to invite them to meet with her.

The office was richly decorated, with bright paintings of flowers lining the walls, overlooking several vases of live plants.

"So what happens now?" Ms. Sizemore asked.

"We hope to speak with Dr. Collins in Knoxville," Allan said. "She's very interested in continuing the research here in the United States."

"In her capacity at a large university, we believe she can make some great strides," Carole added.

"Let's make that happen," Ms. Sizemore said. Then, to her assistant: "Kelly, call Dr. Collins and arrange a face-to-face as soon as we can, preferably tomorrow. We can take the jet and be back in the early afternoon."

Kelly rose from the table and stepped out of the room, cell phone to her ear.

"I don't know that we need to rush things," Allan said. "After all, I'm looking forward to some rest and recuperation time myself."

"I think Kimberly's idea is a good plan," Carole said. "I'm beginning to feel a little stir crazy."

"It's just that I've been running for three weeks, and I need some downtime," Allan said.

"And I'm starting to feel like there's so much more to do to perfect our ectogenesis project. I'm a scientist and a researcher, but all I've been doing is running away. I'm anxious to get involved again," Carole countered.

Allan sensed some of her frustration was directed his way. Things had been quite peaceful before he entered her life, followed by John Sheffield and the ensuing shitstorm that had virtually destroyed the life she knew in Lithuania.

Kelly came back into the room and announced, "We're all set. We'll leave the Dekalb-Peachtree Executive Airport at eight, meet with Dr. Collins at ten and arrive back in town by three."

"Where were you when I tried to book a flight to Lithuania?" Allan asked in an effort to inject a little humor to ease the tension he was feeling with Carole.

The small jet lifted off right on time at eight o'clock. It was snug but comfortable inside the eight-seater, and Ms. Sizemore and Kelly spent most of the time talking about strategy.

They arrived in Knoxville and a limousine took them to the UT campus. Dr. Collins, much calmer and less paranoid, welcomed the entourage to her office. "Allan, I'm so glad we were able to meet again," he said. Then, to Carole, she said, "It's good to see you again as well, Dr. Phillips. Welcome back to the States."

"Thank you, Dr. Collins."

Allan introduced Kimberly Sizemore. "Thank you for meeting with us on such short notice, Dr. Collins," she said.

Dr. Collins smiled broadly. "It's my pleasure."

Ms. Sizemore addressed everyone in the room as if she were addressing a crowd of reporters. "I want you all to know I would like to help support this promising new process. I have contacts in Congress that have already shown interest in writing the Amber Phillips All Children's Birth bill. I want the brightest minds to research this technology right here in the United States

of America. I want our government to approve and endorse your method-
ologies and to set up clinics like the one you had in Lithuania around the
country. And of course, we need to help improve America's adoption and
foster care systems."

Then, to Dr. Collins, she said, "I believe the University of Tennessee
would be a great school to host a research program to take the next steps in
making Dan's dream a reality."

"Thank you, Ms. Sizemore," Dr. Collins said.

"I have some of my people looking into possible grant money as we
speak," she said.

Dr. Collins's eyes lit up like a child's at Christmas.

"I also have some friends who are adept at franchise development who
would like to talk with you about ways to establish incubation clinics around
the country. We hope we can make things happen very quickly."

"You understand a large requirement for this new model is a culture
that embraces adoption," Allan said. "We have to find a way to ensure that
unwanted children are adopted, or the methodology might be seen by some
as more negative than positive."

"I do understand that, Allan," Ms. Sizemore said. "That is an interesting
point—one that will require some dedicated national education. You see,
when the Supreme Court overturned Roe v. Wade, few people realized how
the influx of new, unwanted children would have on the foster care system.
America will have to deal with that regardless of whether ectogenesis exists
or not. It's a tough requirement, but one I think the American people will
rise up to embrace."

"We hope so."

"My God, I feel so energized. I feel like I did in the sixties at the beginning of the movement," Ms. Sizemore said. Then, in a more reserved tone,
she added, "I'd like your approval to begin now. We want to tell the public
that I have talked with you three, and we are all committed deeply to this
new way of life."

Carole nodded her head.

"I'm not so sure," Allan said.

"What's wrong?" Ms. Sizemore asked. "Isn't this what you want?"

Finally, Allan took a deep breath. "Ms. Sizemore, I think you are on the right path. This technology, the incubation process, will make a powerful and lasting impact on our country. Dr. Collins is a great choice to help with the research and development aspects of this project. And I want to believe your motives are pure and true."

"So what is your hesitation?" Carole asked.

"It's that we've all seen public figures who made selfish gains by championing the cause of unborn children. It would be an easy thing to fall into the same trap with the process Dan Carlisle developed."

Ms. Sizemore dwelt on these thoughts for a long time. Then she said, "In the end, only time will reveal my real motives. I just ask that you trust me when I say that I believe this new process will help heal a nation that has been divided far too long. Our nation needs a second chance. Can you trust me?"

"I'll try."

On the flight home, Allan's phone rang.

"Allan, can you talk?" Aunt Julia asked.

"Of course. I'm surprised you didn't send a text."

"No, I feel I need to talk with you about this."

"Okay. Go ahead."

"Allan, I sense disharmony. I don't think Carole is happy here."

"What do you mean?"

"You know I can't be specific. I just sense that her heart longs for another place."

"Wow." He looked at the woman beside him, sleeping with her head against the bulkhead. "Is there anything I can do?"

"She's a strong-willed one," Aunt Julia said.

"Should I follow her?"

"Will you find what you're looking for there?" she asked.

"Probably not. Thank you for letting me know," he said.

"Talk with her, Allan."

The next day, Carole and Allan sat on a bench in Piedmont Park when she turned to him and said, "Allan, I can't stay here."

He breathed in slowly. He had been expecting this conversation since talking with Aunt Julia. "What do you mean?"

"I have no reason to be here in Atlanta, other than to be with you." Tears appeared in her eyes. "If Amber had survived, or if I had an active practice here, I might talk myself into staying. We're no longer running for our lives, but I feel empty inside."

"We could move to Knoxville and work with Dr. Collins," he offered.

"No. It will be years before she gets approval to actually implement the process here in the States. I would feel like my time was being wasted. If I return to Klaipeda, I believe I would be able to legally establish the same process more quickly."

"You believe their government will be more open to these procedures?"

"Yes, I do," she said. "If it takes longer, at least I could continue to help those people with their medical needs. And Dr. Collins has said she will work to support my efforts just as Dan did."

She took his hand. "You know a relationship like ours, created in a crisis, is hard to sustain."

"I've heard that."

"Would you come back with me to Klaipeda?"

Allan thought long and hard to find the answer. "I wish I could, but I can't. I don't belong there."

"What are you going to do?"

"Probably search for a job, maybe down here on the south side. That way, I can continue to develop my friendship with Wes. He was very helpful these last few weeks, you know."

"Yes, he's been a good friend."

Allan thought about the time he had spent with Wes. He had enjoyed the friendship and the sense that he was dealing with something larger than himself. It seemed . . . meaningful. "And who knows. I might give some thought to completing that seminary degree."

Three weeks later, Carole boarded a plane for Klaipeda, Lithuania.

———————————————

"So, how are you holding up?" Wes asked him in a little pizza restaurant a couple of blocks from his church. Allan drank beer. Wes drank Diet Coke. He never drank beer when he was near his church for fear that someone in his congregation might catch him. It wasn't that he thought drinking beer was bad, but that it might confuse some of the members of his church.

"I'll be okay," Allan said. "We move on."

"You know, a lot of good is going to come from the last two months."

"I know. I guess sometimes the healing process hurts a little."

"Well, our country needs to start a dialogue, and I think the process Dan created has opened the door to more of that."

"It's a shame that it cost so much to learn to talk."

They stepped out into an overcast, gloomy winter day in Atlanta. Across the street, a young girl, underdressed for the chill but overdressed for the neighborhood, leaned into the cold weather as she hurried along the sidewalk. Even from a distance, Allan could tell she was pregnant. Somehow, she reminded him of Amanda. As she turned the corner and headed away from them, he felt a bit of hope, for her and for everyone.

AFTERWORD

In 1906, Edward Zim performed the first corneal transplant.

Over sixty-five years later, the Russian ophthalmologist Dr. Svyatoslav N. Fyodorov was treating a young boy whose eyeglasses had shattered, leaving tiny glass fragments in his cornea. After the cornea had healed, Dr. Fyodorov discovered the boy's vision had improved because the cornea had been altered. He began performing cornea surgeries regularly by 1974. In 1978, Dr. Leo Bores brought radial keratotomy to the United States. Today, over seven hundred thousand Lasik surgeries are performed in the US every year.

The first kidney transplant on a dog was performed in Austria in 1902. It wasn't until 1952 that the first successful human kidney transplant was performed. Today, over fifteen thousand kidney transplant operations are performed each year.

Dr. Christiaan Bernard performed the first successful heart transplant in 1967. Today, more than two thousand heart transplants are performed in the United States each year.

Ectogenesis ("living outside") was first suggested by Dr. J.B.S. Haldane a hundred years ago. The concept of an artificial womb was further developed in Aldous Huxley's novel *Brave New World* in 1932. Eighty-five years later, in 2017, a team of researchers at the Children's Hospital of Philadelphia succeeded in incubating a lamb fetus for four weeks in a plastic "bio bag" substituted for a lamb's womb. Similar experiments have been performed since then on younger sheep and on mice.

If we can perform such miraculous surgical feats as the above, is ex vivo ("out of the living") incubation truly an impossibility? While much needs to be considered regarding the morality of ectogenesis, the process offers exciting potential for resolving differences and seeking common ground in the pro-life versus pro-choice debate. Perhaps a part of the problem is we are so intent on insisting our way is right and any alternatives are wrong that we fail to see there just might be a third option.

MORE BOOKS BY BEN A. SHARPTON

The 3rd Option, First Edition
2nd Sight
Camp Fear
The Awakening of Jim Bishop

Word of mouth is crucial for any author to succeed. If you enjoyed *The 3rd Option*, please leave a review online—anywhere you are able—even if it's just a sentence or two. It would make all the difference and would be very much appreciated.

Printed in the USA
CPSIA information can be obtained
at www.ICGtesting.com
LVHW011343280424
778652LV00011B/767